Max gripped her waist and pulled her up off the floor. "We've got to move."

Trying to catch her breath, she took a step and a pain shot through her leg. But now was not the time to worry about that. They were literally under attack.

The smoke was clearing a little so that she could see. But that also meant they could be seen by whoever had attacked them.

A gunshot rang out, and Max pushed her back down to the ground.

"Where did that come from?" she asked.

"I'm not sure, but it sounded like it was from outside. We're going to move farther inside."

Her heart raced as he guided her away from the windows and toward the center of the house. She didn't want to die. She'd been through so much in her life. She wasn't going to give up now. She could handle this, too.

Rachel Dylan writes inspirational romantic suspense. Although a Georgia girl at heart, she traded in the sunny South for the snowy Midwest. She lives in Michigan with her husband and five furkids—two dogs and three cats. She's an animal lover and enjoys adding furry friends to her stories. You can find Rachel at racheldylan.com.

Books by Rachel Dylan

Love Inspired Suspense

Out of Hiding
Expert Witness

EXPERT WITNESS

RACHEL DYLAN

HARLEQUIN® LOVE INSPIRED® SUSPENSE

Recycling programs
for this product may
not exist in your area.

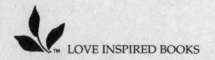

™ LOVE INSPIRED BOOKS

ISBN-13: 978-0-373-67706-1

Expert Witness

Copyright © 2015 by Rachel Dylan

www.Harlequin.com

Printed in U.S.A.

The Lord is my light and my salvation; whom shall I fear?
The Lord is the strength of my life;
of whom shall I be afraid?
—Psalms 27:1

To my mom—the strongest woman I've ever known. I love you.

Many thanks to my fabulous agent, Sarah Younger,
for being my fierce advocate,
and my amazing editor Emily Rodmell
for believing in my work.

ONE

"All rise." The bailiff's deep voice echoed through the crowded Atlanta courtroom.

Sydney Berry took a deep breath and stepped down from the witness stand. Unfortunately, her expert testimony as a forensic artist in the murder trial of businessman Kevin Diaz wasn't over. She'd have to come back tomorrow and testify about her sessions with the eyewitness and the drawing she'd created of the suspect. The goal—to get the sketch of the suspect introduced into evidence. It would bolster the eyewitness testimony to have the contemporaneous drawing in front of the jury.

If the defense attorney was able to tear apart her testimony, the prosecution's case would be severely weakened. And a guilty man likely would walk free. She refused to let that happen.

She walked out of the courtroom doors, and then the other bailiff standing outside nodded to her, indicating she was on her own. *Dear*

God, please give me the strength to get through this. Let my testimony help the jury so that justice may be done for the murder of an innocent woman.

"Ms. Berry!" A male voice rang out down the courthouse hallway.

The last thing she wanted to do right now was deal with the press. She'd refused every media inquiry thus far, and she would do the same again today. Because of Kevin Diaz's position in the community, the local Atlanta media were having a field day covering the trial.

"No comment." She turned around and came face to face with a tall man in a dark suit and a navy checkered tie. No, he didn't look like the press. He had to be a Fed. His dark brown hair was cut short, and his eyes were a striking deep green.

"I'm not a reporter," he said. "Please let me escort you to your vehicle, and I'll explain."

She took a step, and he followed her.

She turned to him. "Who are you?"

He looked her in the eyes. "I'm US Marshal Max Preston."

Close. She had figured him for FBI. Having dealt with the FBI quite a bit in her line of work, she knew its style, and he fit it perfectly down to the gun she caught a glimpse of on his right hip. Though she wasn't accustomed to consulting for the US Marshals, they were obviously built from the same mold.

"As you can tell, I'm a bit preoccupied right now with this trial." She reached into her pocket for her business card. "Here's my card. Contact me and we can set up a consultation. But it will probably be a few weeks before I can fit it into my schedule." When he refused the card, she pocketed it and pushed open the courthouse door. The summer heat of Atlanta hit her, and she already felt her hair starting to frizz.

"I know this is bad timing, but I need five minutes," he said, following her outside.

The persistent marshal wasn't taking no for an answer. They walked down the courthouse steps on to the sidewalk.

"Really, sir, this isn't a good time."

He touched her arm. "It's important, Ms. Berry. I wouldn't come to you like this otherwise, but I really need to talk to you. Now."

Then she heard car wheels screeching loudly. Looking toward the street, she saw a dark SUV barreling down the road in their direction at top speed. Instinctively, she took a step back.

The tinted window rolled down, and the sound of gunshots exploded through the air. Before she could duck, she found herself hitting the sidewalk hard with the faint taste of blood in her mouth.

Screams and mass chaos erupted around her. As she looked up, trying to determine what had happened, she realized that the US marshal with the bright green eyes was on top of her, shielding her body with his own. He had knocked her down. Probably saving her life.

"That's what I wanted to talk to you about," he said quietly in her ear. "Are you okay?" He lifted his weight off her and his eyes scanned her from head to toe, as if looking for signs of injury.

"I'm fine." She paused, trying to catch her breath. "Wait a minute. You think those bullets were meant for me?"

He gently pulled her up off the ground and wrapped one arm around her shoulder to steady her. "Unfortunately, I do. I need to get you to a secure location. Now."

As police officers swarmed around them, he flashed his marshal's badge and was able to get through the crowd. He pulled one of the officers aside. "Neil, we need to talk."

"What happened here?" the officer asked him.

"Drive-by shooting. Approximately five shots fired. Two men, driver and passenger."

"Did you get a visual on either?"

"Negative, but they were in a black Chevy SUV—model year late nineties. I'm assuming it was stolen, and they're probably dumping the vehicle as we speak."

"You're probably right about that."

"Look, Neil, call me if you need anything else, but right now I need to get this witness out of here. When it's safe, we can provide official statements. Please keep me in the loop. You have my info."

The officer nodded at Max and then looked at her closely. Recognition spread across his face. He must have been following the Diaz trial. "Of course. Whatever you need, Max."

Max took her arm and led her down the street away from the courthouse. "I should try to explain why I came here today. I think you're in more danger than you could know."

"With that lead in, I guess you already know me pretty well."

"Yes, I do, Ms. Berry."

"Please, call me Sydney. After you saved my life I feel like the formalities are a bit much. Can I call you Max?"

"Of course."

"So, what's going on exactly?"

He gently touched her back and guided her to his car, which he'd parked in the lot down the block from the courthouse. He opened the door, and she got into the nondescript gray sedan. Only then did he start to explain.

"I used to work in the gang unit at the FBI." He paused. "But I came here today to warn you that there was chatter amongst the gang networks about you. Have you ever heard of the East River gang?"

"Yeah, they're pretty notorious." She wasn't ready to provide her specific knowledge of the East River gang to this man she just met. Even if he had saved her life, she thought it better to proceed with caution. That was the way she lived now.

"Well, I put two and two together and I think the East River gang has decided to go after you because of your testimony here in the case against Kevin Diaz."

"Kevin Diaz is a businessman with multiple thriving companies. What connection could he possibly have to the East River gang?" She kept her voice steady even as her mind started to play out the implications of this new piece of information.

"Kevin's cousin is Lucas Jones, who just happens to also be one of the power players in East River."

She looked over at him. "Wow. I had no idea they were related." She paused. "And now you think they're coming after me because of the family connection?"

"I'll be honest with you. I'm one of the only ones who believes that Lucas Jones would take action for his estranged cousin. Most of my former FBI colleagues believe that the two of them aren't on speaking terms. But I do and that's why I'm here. I had a feeling that East River would retaliate against you and today's events only confirm my hunch."

"Are you sure?"

He kept his eyes on the road. "I felt pretty strongly about it before, but you were almost gunned down in broad daylight outside the courthouse. So, yes, it's a threat I take seriously. The US Marshals' office is taking it seriously."

"What does all of this mean?"

"It means that for the time being you'll be in my protective custody. It was one thing when you were just testifying in a murder trial against Kevin Diaz. But circumstances have changed. If you're a target of the East River gang because of your testimony that impacts everything. First and foremost your personal safety. When you agreed to testify as an expert witness for the state, it wasn't under these circumstances."

· She took a second and looked out the window as they drove. "Is all this really necessary?"

"Most people are thankful for the protection, Ms. Berry."

I can take care of myself, she thought. "It's Sydney, remember? And it's not that I'm not thankful. It's just that I'm having a hard time processing all of this. I'm not exactly used to being shot at when testifying in a major trial. Not to mention being told that I'm going to have my every move shadowed by someone I just met. I just need a few minutes to think it all through."

He nodded. "If you decide to continue to testify tomorrow, I'll make sure you are able to safely arrive and finish your testimony. Then we'll determine the next steps after that."

"What do you mean *if*? Why wouldn't I testify? I already committed to it."

"That was before you knew about the danger to your life. The prosecutor will have to talk to you about the risks involved. And then we'll need to lie low until there's a proper threat assessment conducted on the risk to your life from the East River gang."

She couldn't believe what she was hearing. "Wait. Are you talking about putting me into the witness-protection program?"

"That would be premature at this juncture."

"But you're not ruling it out?"

"I never rule out any course of action. Doing

so is the easiest way to get you or someone else killed. But the lead prosecutor and state's attorney are going to be fully briefed on the current security issues, and they may seek that route for you. Especially after what just happened."

"Unbelievable." She lived a solitary life so she didn't have to worry about a family, but this marshal was throwing her a curve. Granted, he was just doing his job, but that didn't mean she felt comfortable with him taking over. She was a private person. She'd only trusted a man once before, and she shuddered thinking about him.

"I know this is difficult for you. If it makes you feel any better, I'll do everything I can to keep you safe and try and give you as much space as is reasonable."

"I guess I understand. But how could the state not have known about this connection to the East River gang?"

"Since there isn't any proven contact or links between the two cousins, I don't think the state believed this was a relevant issue. Lucas thought Kevin sold out by working in corporate America. Or at least that's the story that's on the streets."

"But you're skeptical?"

"Yeah. I'm not doubting that there's friction between the two of them, but I don't buy for a minute that Kevin Diaz is completely on the up and up. The FBI is investigating his operations trying to find any other ties to East River or organized crime. However, it's not their top priority. Like I said, I was the one driving that charge, and now that I'm gone it's less of a focus. Regardless, in my opinion East River made clear today that they don't want you to testify."

"But I've already started my testimony."

"And they don't want you to finish it," he shot back. "You've only gotten through the preliminary questions. Nothing you've said so far will hurt Diaz. It's the rest of your testimony that would be problematic for him. So for tonight we have to be on lockdown. I'm taking you to a safe house in the area."

"I'll need something to wear for court tomorrow."

"Don't worry. All of that will be taken care of. We have a fully stocked safe house, and if need be we can send out for any additional necessities."

She leaned her head back against the seat and closed her eyes for a second trying to steady her ever escalating nerves. She liked to be in control, and right now things were spiraling quickly into a place she didn't like to be. *Lord, I need You now.*

"Are you all right?" he asked.

"Yes. How much farther until we reach our destination?"

"It's just outside the city, so only a few more minutes."

"Sorry to sound impatient."

He glanced over at her. "You were just shot at. You have every right to feel a mix of emotions. I'm actually quite impressed at how you've held yourself together."

She wanted to change the subject and take the focus off of her. "Are you from around here?" she asked.

"I'm from Chicago, but I've lived all over working for the FBI. For the past few years I worked out of the Atlanta field office. And now as a marshal, I've been assigned to the Northern District of Georgia."

"I like living in Atlanta," she said.

The car suddenly swerved, stopping her from continuing her thought. What was going on?

"Hold on," he said loudly.

She gripped the console.

Then he slammed on the brakes.

Max's day was going from bad to worse. If he hadn't gotten to the courthouse when he had, his witness might have been killed—gunned down in broad daylight. And now a man stood waving his arms right in front of his car in the middle of the road.

Max had to swerve to keep from hitting him. But it was close. And now his senses were screaming that something was terribly off. They were winding through the suburbs on the way to the safe house. What was this man doing?

He thought of Sydney. How much more could she handle today? She certainly hadn't signed up for being a target of the East River gang. His years in the FBI gang unit had shown him just how ruthless a group like East River could be.

"Are you going to get out and see what he needs?" she asked.

They sat in the car, not moving, as the man approached. Max estimated him to be in his forties, approximately six feet tall and two hundred pounds. He definitely didn't look like a damsel in distress.

"What's wrong?" she asked Max.

"I don't like this."

"He probably needs help." She reached over and grabbed his arm. "We can't just ignore him."

"Stay in the car, okay?"

Before she could answer, he checked his sidearm and then opened the door.

And that's when the man lunged forward. The attacker was fast, but Max was faster.

Sydney screamed, but Max stayed focused on the threat in front of him. But when a gunshot went off, he instinctively turned to look. And there was Sydney wrestling another man with a gun.

He didn't have time to do a thorough analysis of the situation, so he quickly launched into action. When his attacker landed a blow that connected hard with his jaw, pain shot through his head. But it wasn't enough to lay him out. There was no way was he going to lose his first official witness as a US Marshal. With a swift uppercut he made contact with the attacker's face. Calling on his martial arts training, he followed with a precise kick to the ribs. His assailant landed on the ground with a resounding thud.

He drew his gun and turned, ready to take the shot to save Sydney's life. But somehow she had gotten the other guy on his knees and the man's gun was now in her hand. How in the world had she managed that? "Keep that gun on him, Sydney."

"You don't have to worry about that," she said.

He pulled out his handcuffs and secured the original assailant. Then he walked over to her.

The other man was on his knees with his hands in the air. He pulled out a second pair of cuffs from his jacket and put them on the perpetrator.

He would need to call this in ASAP, but he also needed to get Sydney to safety. What if others were coming? These guys could have been waiting for them. Which meant additional threats could be in the area.

He pulled out his cell and put in a call. Backup should only be a few minutes away. That would give him a moment with the suspects. He read them their rights since he didn't want to get caught in a legal snafu, and then he looked at the first man.

"Who sent you?"

"I'm not talkin'." The man's blue eyes weren't filled with fear but determination. Clearly he was a hired gun.

Max walked over to where Sydney stood beside the other man. Her auburn hair had come loose from her ponytail. "You sure you're okay?" She looked shaken as she gripped her hands together, but after a moment answered him calmly.

"Yes."

He turned his attention to the man. "You got anything to say?"

The guy grunted, and Max took that as a no. No surprises there.

As they held the men at gunpoint he leaned in to her. "Where in the world did you learn to incapacitate an attacker like that?" He guessed her to be only about five feet four, but she was a powerhouse.

Her brown eyes were wide as she looked up at him. "Self-defense classes."

"That looked like a whole lot more than self-defense class."

She shifted her weight from one foot to the other. "I'd rather not talk about it."

He was intrigued. Sydney Berry had secrets. And if he was going to be able to keep her safe, he probably needed to find them out. But at the moment he was just glad that her first secret actually worked to their advantage.

He was kicking himself for taking his eyes off of her earlier. She was his first and only priority. Granted, she wasn't officially in the Witness Security Program, known commonly as witness protection, but he had been tasked to keep her safe until everything could be sorted out.

Sirens sounded in the distance. He looked at her. "Why don't you get in the car? I'll handle this, and then we can be on our way."

She frowned but then got into the sedan.

A moment later the local police arrived, and Max filled them in on the specifics. He'd also looped in his FBI contact. Then he made the call he was dreading. Reporting this incident to his boss, Deputy Elena Sanchez, was hardly the way to make a good first impression, but he had no choice.

Then finally he was ready to hit the road with Sydney. But not to the original safe house. That was too risky now.

He wouldn't feel even an ounce better until Sydney had safely completed her testimony in the morning. And even then the threat of the East River gang still loomed large.

Once they'd been driving for a few minutes, he decided to break the silence. "Want to talk about what happened back there?"

"You think those men were connected to East River or someone else associated with Diaz?"

He decided it best to be open and honest with her about the threat. "I think East River has put a hit out on you."

"I had a feeling you were going to say that," she said.

He saw her look out the window and take note of her surroundings. "I know it seems like I'm driving in the other direction now, but given what just happened we're going to an alternative safe house."

"But we're not staying there long?"

"No. After you testify we'll go to another location. This is just for tonight. We have a list of safe house options already planned for you."

"I guess I don't get much of a say in this, huh?"

"You always have a say, but you should know that I have your best interests in mind. Also, I'm sorry about what happened back there, however, I'm thankful that you were able to defend yourself."

"Me, too," she said quietly.

He looked over at her. As she stared out the window he could see the tension tightening her features. He tried a different topic of conversation. "How long have you been a sketch artist?"

She turned to look at him, and her shoulders immediately seemed to relax. "I've been drawing forever, but I started taking it seriously during college. I didn't finish school and instead took art classes with my tuition money. Then I started with small jobs and it grew from there. Referrals are very important in my business. But I do more than just draw faces. That's what you think of when you think of a sketch artist. I'm a forensic artist. I can do a lot more, like crime-scene reenactments and stuff like that."

"I imagine the work comes and goes." He wanted to engage in conversation to try to calm his own building nerves, as well.

"Yes. I've been very busy as of late, but those first few years were tough. I took other odd jobs to make ends meet. I worked at a library for a bit and as a server at a restaurant. All to pursue my real dream." She shrugged. "With all the high-tech advancements, the field is changing a lot, it's really exciting. Computers can do a lot, but there's still something to be said about a human hand."

"I'm a big fan of using technology in investigations. I had an experience with a traditional sketch artist in the past who wasn't on point." That was an understatement, but he didn't think it was the best time to go into his misgivings about sketch artists right now.

"Don't get me wrong. The technology for doing things like facial reconstructions or accident simulations is absolutely amazing," she replied. "But I still trust my abilities to use pencil and paper and sketch based on the eyewitness interview for the purposes of identification."

He didn't reply because it only would have led to an argument that he didn't think she would want to have right now.

"You said you were at the FBI before. How long have you been a marshal?"

He didn't really want to give an exact answer. "Not very long." He could feel her gaze on him as he drove.

"Hey, don't tell me I'm your first witness."

He smiled. "Okay, I won't tell you that."

"Wow." She blew out a breath. "I *am* your first witness."

"That's true, but I'd been with the FBI for a decade. It's not like I'm new to law enforcement, so I'm not a true rookie."

"I can imagine that working as an FBI agent in the gang unit is a lot different than guarding a witness, though."

"Don't give it another thought. You're safe now, and you'll stay that way."

"No offense, but we just met. You're asking me to put a lot of faith in you."

"I know. But that's the way it has to be. No one else on our team has the same knowledge of the threats to you like I do. I'm thankful that I got assigned to your case and was able to connect the dots, or this afternoon might have ended very differently." He paused as he pointed to a house up ahead. "We're here on the right."

"This looks like a regular neighborhood."

"That's exactly the point. We're trying to blend."

He'd actually never been to this safe house before during his training, but he was getting the idea that they were all generally the same.

This was a two-story house, painted a pale blue on a nice-size lot.

He pulled the sedan all the way into the driveway and stopped the car.

"Can I get out?" she asked.

"Yes, but first let me just do a quick security check. You stay here and keep the doors locked."

Before she could answer he had jogged up to the front door and opened it. He quickly surveyed the house, conducting a security sweep. Satisfied it was all clear he went back outside to get Sydney. Her expression appeared unreadable as she sat in the passenger's seat. He really wanted to know what was going in that head of hers.

He opened the car door for her, and she stepped out bedside him. She was a pretty woman, no doubt, with a simple and natural beauty about her. But she gave off a very strong vibe. One that said loudly, "Back off."

"This way," he said. He took her arm and escorted her to the front door, even though he got the feeling she didn't appreciate him invading her personal space. "Another marshal will be over in a bit with dinner and everything you'll need for tonight and tomorrow."

"You aren't leaving, are you?" she asked as she made direct eye contact.

"No. I just didn't want you to think we were going to be totally shut off from the outside world without the things you would need."

"What I really need is to be at my own home."

"I understand. Let's get through your testimony in the morning, and then we can re-evaluate."

"I'll hold you to that."

He walked over to where she stood in the living room. "I promise. And I won't make you promises I can't keep. I hate it when people do that to me and—"

A loud crash rocked the room as glass flew against his body. His face burned and he felt blood trickling down his cheek. Smoke surrounded him. He dove toward Sydney, hoping it wouldn't be too late.

TWO

Smoke filled Sydney's lungs as she tried to draw a breath. Max was on the ground beside her, and his face was bleeding. Then she noticed the shards of glass littering the floor around them, and realized he must have been hit by one.

Max gripped her waist and pulled her up off the floor. "We've got to move."

Trying to catch her breath, she took a step and pain shot through her leg. Blood covered her right arm as it throbbed at her side. But now was not the time to worry about that. They were literally under attack.

The smoke was clearing a little so that she could see. But that also meant they could be seen by whoever had attacked them.

A gunshot rang out, and Max pushed her back down to the ground.

"Where did that come from?" she asked.

"I'm not sure, but it sounded like it was from

outside. We're going to move farther in to the interior of the house."

Her heart raced as, on their hands and knees, he guided her further away from the windows and toward the center of the house. *I don't want to die.* She'd been through so much in her life. She wasn't going to give up now. She could handle this, too. Taking a deep breath, she crawled toward the bathroom door.

Pulling her in, he shut the door and wrapped his arms around her shoulders. She couldn't help but flinch as he touched her—but it wasn't from the pain.

"What hurts?" he asked.

"My arm and my leg. But I don't think it's too serious." She paused and looked up at him. "Your face is bleeding." She reached up and touched his cheek, trying to determine where the blood was coming from. "Looks like you got hit on the side of your face with a piece of glass."

"Yeah, I think it's just a nick. I'll—"

His remark was cut short by a deep male voice that rang throughout the house. "Anyone here?"

Max put his fingers to his lips indicating that she should not respond.

"Preston, are you there? It's Davies."

She watched as Max's shoulders visibly dropped. "He's one of ours," he told her.

"Back here, Davies."

Max helped her to her feet and opened the bathroom door.

Through the clearing smoke she saw a man and woman both dressed in suits approaching them. "The suspect was able to flee," the tall blond man said. "We wanted to make sure the package was secure."

"Are you okay?" the woman asked.

"A bit sore," Sydney replied. "But I guess it could've been much worse."

The woman looked at Max. "So, what happened?"

Max wiped the blood from his face with a handkerchief. "They broke through the window with a smoke bomb. Probably planned to use that as a diversion to grab Sydney."

The blond man stepped closer. "Ms. Berry, I'm sorry, ma'am. We should've introduced ourselves. I'm Phillip Davies and this is Elena Sanchez. We work with Max and are both deputies with the US Marshals."

They shook hands with Sydney.

"I'm sorry to rush you," Elena said. "But we need to address any immediate medical issues, and then you two need to move. It's not safe here." As she ushered them down the hall, she said, "Ms. Berry, I've got a bag for you in our car. Given these attacks, we have to assume our system has been compromised in some way. An electronic security breach is unlikely, but it's more possible in my mind than a mole within the US Marshals."

She led them into the living room with the blown-in window and assessed the surroundings. Then she turned to Sydney. "Ms. Berry, you're going to be taken to a safe house that wasn't in the list of those assigned to you. Deputy Preston, this is officially need-to-know right now. Meaning you, Deputy Davies and I are the only three people to know the locations of any future safe houses. Keeping the circle this small will ensure Ms. Berry's safety."

Sydney noted Elena's take-charge attitude. She liked the tall dark-haired marshal with welcoming brown eyes already.

Elena took her arm. "I'll get you safely to the vehicle while they secure this area. Deputy Preston, we'll switch cars and you'll take mine."

"Roger that," Max said.

Elena led her out the front door and to the driveway. "Are you sure you're not hurt?"

"Not badly. Probably just superficial wounds."

"I've got a med kit in the car. I'll take a look at your arm."

"Thank you." She paused and tried to gather her thoughts. "Am I still going to be able to testify in the morning? Because I think that—"

"Wait a second, Ms. Berry." Holding up her hand, Elena cut her off. "Since you've been sworn in as a witness already, you shouldn't say anything about your testimony. I don't want you to get in trouble with the court. I understand that you want to testify, and we will do our best to make sure that happens. Deputy Preston will continuously conduct a threat assessment, and it will ultimately be his call as to whether it is safe to bring you into the courtroom tomorrow morning."

"Can I ask you something?"

"Sure." Elena removed the medical kit from the trunk. "Sit in the car while I see to your arm. Ask away."

"How long have you known Max?" She tried not to yelp as Elena pushed up her sleeve to reveal a nasty cut that was still oozing blood. Elena opened the kit and started to clean her wound.

"Just about a month."

"A month? That's it?"

"He's recently transferred from the FBI. But don't worry. He has a stellar reputation. Word is that he took on the toughest assignments in the gang unit, including a stint of deep undercover years ago that proved to be invaluable in a number of convictions." Elena finished cleaning the cut and then bandaged it. "So you should have no concerns about him."

"How long have you been with the US Marshals?"

"For quite some time." Elena gently pulled Sydney's sleeve down over the bandage. "And I wouldn't change a thing. Best decision I ever made. I thank God every day for opening up the opportunity for me."

She received a measure of comfort from Elena's words. If it weren't for the Lord, she wouldn't have made it through the past few years. And now she needed Him more than ever.

"I'm sure Deputy Preston has mentioned that given the attacks, the prosecutor and the FBI will want to talk to you about your safety and your options. One of those options is witness protection. I just didn't want you to be surprised when those discussions started in case he hadn't given you all those details."

"I understand," she said softly.

"Here, take these." Elena handed her a package with two pain relievers and a bottle of water.

"Thank you."

"The perimeter is secure," Max reported as

he approached the vehicle with Davies beside him. Sydney had to admit the two men were quite a formidable presence.

"Great. Then you two should get going," Elena said. "Here's the address." She handed Max a piece of paper.

Sydney shook Elena's hand. "Thank you for everything."

"You're more than welcome. Deputy Preston, she's in your hands now."

"Understood."

Elena gave Max the car keys, and they spoke in hushed tones for a minute. Sydney couldn't make out what they were saying, but she knew enough to understand that she was in danger. A danger that was coming from multiple fronts.

She pushed down the fear deep inside of her. Every fact indicated that Max Preston was a professional who would do his best to keep her safe. But her insecurities and mistrust ran deep.

Max got in the car and started the engine. Then he looked over at her. "I know you want to testify, but I think that would be a very bad idea until we get more security in place."

"How would that work?"

"We'd have the prosecutor ask the judge for a short continuance based on the very real threats and actions that have been taken against you."

"We don't even know who is behind all of this."

"You're right. It could be people working directly for Kevin Diaz. Or it could be the gang. Or both. But all of the signs point to East River. If Diaz had his own hired guns, I don't think they would've gone about it in the same way." He checked behind him and pulled out of the driveway.

"Wouldn't it be better for me to testify and get it over with? That would at least neutralize one of the threats. After I testify the sketch I did and my testimony are in front of the jury. Even if Diaz and East River are sending people after me, it won't matter at that point."

"Except for revenge."

She shuddered at the thought. "I think their primary goal would be to stop me from testifying in the first place. Which is why I need to testify in the morning. The sketch I created will help substantiate the testimony from the eyewitness. The prosecution is concerned about how the eyewitness will hold up on the stand. But if my sketch is entered into evidence, that will provide support for the reliability of the witness."

He smiled. "You're a very tough woman, Sydney, and I respect your tenacity. But my job is to protect you. I'd feel a lot better if we were authorized to have additional security in and around the courtroom. I think we'll get it, but we'll need a short continuance from the judge to get that all set up."

She prayed that she could trust this man. "So what kind of delay are you thinking?"

"Just a day or so."

"And for now?"

"We go to the new safe house. Then we'll have some dinner and settle in for the night."

She noticed him looking in the rearview mirror. She turned around but didn't see any cars. "Did you see something?"

"No. Just being extra cautious."

"Do you have a theory about who that was at the first safe house?"

"I have a lot of theories. But it would be logical to hypothesize that all of these threats today have been from the East River gang. That's what I think is most likely. If Diaz is involved, I think it's through his connection to East River. He's a powerful man with a lot of resources."

"How closely have you looked at the possible connection between Diaz and his cousin Lucas Jones?"

"Not deeply enough. While you were outside with Elena I put in a quick call to a former colleague at the FBI asking him to work that angle. The shooting at the courthouse was something the gang would definitely do. Your testimony threatens to convict Diaz of murder.

Someone with his power and influence can't be underestimated. Even if Diaz and Jones aren't on the best terms, Diaz could've provided him with a huge payout to get the job done."

"I agree with you on that."

"I know it's hard, but just try to relax. We'll be at the next safe house soon."

But how could she when his eyes kept darting to the rearview mirror?

Morning light filtered through the closed blinds as Max paced the first floor of the safe house, clenching and unclenching his fists in an effort to calm his nerves. Fortunately, last night had been uneventful. Not that he'd slept much. It had stormed most of the evening. According to the weather report, there was no end in sight to the line of powerful storms moving across the South. The strong summer rain pounded down outside and thunder roared.

He'd decided that even though she was determined to testify, it would be too dangerous to get Sydney into the courthouse today. His first order of business then was to talk to the prosecutor and the FBI to try to get a security-based continuance. Given the circumstances he had no doubt that the judge would grant it.

When he walked into the kitchen Sydney sat at the table with a cup of coffee. Her long hair was loose and flowed down around her shoulders. She was attractive, but she wasn't just a pretty face. He'd seen her take down that attacker with strength and determination.

Sensing his presence, she looked up. "Good morning."

"Were you able to sleep?"

"Not very well." She paused. "But probably a bit more than you did."

"I'm able to function on very little sleep."

"From all those years undercover in the gang unit?"

"Well, that's a big part of it." He paused. "Elena must have told you about my background."

"Yes, she did. She spoke very highly of your track record at the FBI."

"After a while, you learn how to operate without much sleep."

"Whatever it is, I thank God that I'm still alive today." She looked up at him.

"You're a believer, I take it?" he asked.

She nodded. "My faith is tied to who I am. I honestly wouldn't have made it to this point in my life if it hadn't been for my faith."

He supposed he shouldn't have been surprised. She was an artist, after all, and in his experience they were emotional, empathetic. Both things he was not. Things he had rejected years ago. In fact, he was the complete opposite. Some people even called him cold and calculating. But it came with the turf, and it made him good at his job.

She stood, walked to the cabinet and pulled out a cup. "Coffee?"

"Thank you. Black, please."

She poured him a cup and then turned around, her eyes full of life. "I'm not judging you, but I take it by your silence that you don't share my views on faith?"

He sat down and wondered for a moment how he should answer. The last thing he wanted to do was alienate this woman. But he also had to be truthful. "I'm not a religious person—at least not anymore. I rely more on a rational and scientific approach to life these days."

She smiled. "Saying you are or aren't religious carries a lot of connotations with it."

He sipped his coffee and considered his response carefully. He decided to take the direct approach. "I don't go to church, Sydney."

She cocked her head to the side. "Is that how you were raised?"

"Actually, no. My parents were both churchgoers. I was expected to attend church with them every Sunday until I left home to go off to college. When I was young I considered myself a Christian and felt good about it. I enjoyed going to church. As I grew up, though, I started having second thoughts. In my experience, just because people went to church didn't make them better people. Actions speak a lot louder than words. By the time I got to college I had a healthy and logical skepticism about the entire thing. I took a few classes on different religions in college. I viewed them in the same way as I did my other coursework in philosophy."

"I wasn't raised by people of faith. My dad was never in the picture, and my mom didn't see any point in going to church. But when I found God, my life changed forever." She put down her cup and smiled at him. "Don't worry. I'm not going to try to convince you to change your mind. I believe we each find our way in our own time. But I do believe with all my heart that God is watching over us right now. Both of us."

"If that makes you feel better, then I'm all for it."

She shook her head. "It's not just about making me feel better. I realize you don't think this, but God is not imaginary. Just because you can't see something doesn't mean it doesn't exist."

He shrugged his shoulders. His phone rang, and he was glad to have an out from the awkward conversation. The last thing he needed was a lecture on faith. He knew better. He'd lived through a childhood with parents who acted one way on Sunday morning and a totally different way the rest of the week.

"Deputy Preston," he answered.

"It's Elena. We have a problem."

"What?" Immediately his pulse started to thump.

"I just got off a conference call with local police and the FBI. Kevin Diaz has violated the terms of his bail. He's not in Atlanta, and no one on his staff or his legal team knows exactly where he is. Or if they do know, they aren't saying."

"What? You can't be serious. How in the world did that happen?"

"His lawyers are trying to say there has been some sort of miscommunication about his schedule. They're pushing back hard that there's nothing wrong here, and that Kevin will be located promptly. But the judge has been informed and is not happy. The FBI will start to look for him along with the police," Elena said.

He didn't need to hear any more. "I'm implementing the alternate strategy we discussed yesterday."

"Yes. That's the best thing to do given the circumstances," she said.

"Roger that."

"You should move soon. I'll keep you posted on any developments on Diaz." She paused. "And watch your back, Max."

He hung up and looked over at Sydney. Her eyes were focused on him like a laser beam.

"What's going on? And don't sugarcoat it. I need to know the truth. I deserve to know the truth."

He agreed. It was better to just say it. "Kevin Diaz has violated his bail. No one seems to know exactly where he is."

Her eyes widened as she sat for a moment in silence.

"I'm sorry. But this means we've got to get out of here as soon as you can get ready," he said.

"What's the plan you were talking about implementing?"

"We're leaving Atlanta."

"Whoa." She stood up and walked over to him. "Are you talking about witness protection?"

"Not yet. Just protective custody for now, but we are going to leave the city. It will be safer that way. And the location is not attached to you in our electronic system, so we have that angle covered just in case there's any risk of a security breach."

"But I can't just abandon my life."

"I realize your apprehension. This is only a temporary solution until we figure out exactly what's going on and the level of all the threats against you."

"Temporary? How can you be so sure?"

He sighed. "I can't. But for now we've got to start mobilizing. Go get ready and gather up what little stuff you have. Then we'll get out of here."

She nodded and walked away, and he resisted the urge to go to her. He needed to stay alert. Focused and determined to protect Sydney Berry at all cost. Her words about God watching over them were nagging at him, though. It wasn't God, but hard work by the US Marshals that was keeping her safe.

And where had God been when he had needed Him in the dark days of his youth? When his dad had been gone for days on end doing who knew what and his mom hadn't been able to put together a coherent sentence because she had been so strung out on prescription meds?

Abandoning that line of thought, he gathered up his stuff, and within half an hour they were on the road. The rain had gotten worse and lightning streaked through the sky. He had to drive much slower than he would've preferred given the circumstances.

"Where are we headed?" Sydney asked him when they had been on the road a while.

"We aren't going to stay in one spot too long. We're going to use the small Georgia towns to our advantage. First stop is a town called Pikeville in south Georgia."

"Never heard of it."

"I hadn't, either, until this case. It's a rural area, though. I know that much."

"And what will we do there?" she asked.

"Lie low."

"Doing what?"

"You sure do ask a lot of questions."

She shrugged. "I think I have the right to do so. And small towns can be difficult. Everyone knows everyone. We'll stick out."

"That's why we'll have our cover story and never stay long enough for anyone to start asking the really tough questions."

She sighed. "When are you planning to share the cover story with me?"

He dreaded this explanation because he knew she wouldn't like it. "I need to explain something to you. This cover is just temporary and specific to our current strategy. If the situation changes and you are formally placed in the Witness Security Program—otherwise known as witness protection—your cover would be entirely different. In fact, it wouldn't be a cover but a new life. A new name, a new past, a new everything."

"I don't want a new life. I already told you that. I've worked so hard to have the life I have now."

Loud thunder boomed, and he saw her flinch. Something deeper than what he had tapped into so far was going on with her. It wasn't just the Diaz case that had her edgy. "I get that. I just didn't want there to be any confusion between what's happening now and what could possibly happen in the future."

"Now that you've gotten that off your chest, let's get back to my original question. Our cover."

"Right." He glanced over at her. She sure was feisty this morning. "We're working on a special story on Southern towns for a national magazine. If anyone asks, we'll just say that we can't reveal the identity of the magazine because the feature is a surprise. The less we have to say to anyone the better."

"Where will we stay?"

"Mostly hotels or inns. We're just traveling through. Getting what we need for our story and then moving on."

"So we're coworkers?"

"Exactly. And just to make it simple, I'll call you Syd instead of Sydney, and we'll switch last names. So you're Syd Preston and I'm Max Berry. Once again, if you were to go into the program, you'd have a completely different name. These names are only temporary to get us through the first town."

She let out a breath. "I'd rather not even think about that right now."

His phone rang, and he put it on speaker as he drove. "Deputy Preston," he answered.

"It's Elena."

"Hey, you're on speaker with Sydney."

"Great. How are you holding up, Sydney?"

"Given the circumstances, I guess I'm all right."

"Hang in there. You've got a team of people around you protecting and supporting you. Don't forget that."

"Thank you," Sydney said.

"Any more word on Kevin Diaz?" Max asked.

"They're still searching for him. His people are busy with the PR spin. One of his staffers claims he had to attend a board meeting for one of the nonprofit corporations he works with. But that just may be an excuse to try to buy Diaz time. Regardless, the terms of his bail were clear. He violated those terms, and I imagine once he's located his bail will be revoked."

Max huffed out a breath. "What a piece of

work that guy is. He thinks he's so powerful that he's above the law, and the normal rules don't apply to him. Any further intel on ballistics from the courthouse shooting?"

"Still waiting. At this point there's no evidence tying Kevin to the shooting. If I had to speculate I'd say it's more likely that it was East River acting on Kevin's behalf. Regardless, neither threat is neutralized, so we stay the course with Sydney."

"Give me a call with any developments."

"Will do. Stay safe. I just looked at the weather radar and there are severe storms all around the area. It's making the drive around here treacherous, and it looks even worse in your direction."

"Understood." He disconnected the call and looked over at Sydney. She sat quietly, her hands folded in her lap, a hard-to-read expression on her face. "What's on your mind?"

"How quickly this whole thing has spiraled out of control. I can't say I'm surprised that Diaz thought he didn't have to abide by the conditions of his bail. But with all his resources I'm sure he'll wiggle out of it somehow."

They drove for a long time in silence while lightning lit up the sky that was growing ever darker with storms.

"If Diaz's exact location is unknown, do you

think it's possible that he could come after me personally?" she asked.

"No, that's far too risky, especially given the latest events. But I do think he may send some hired guns after you. Or, if I'm right about the connection between the cousins, the East River gang may just do the dirty work. Eliminate the threat you pose forever."

"And by eliminate you mean kill."

"Yes, but as I've said I'm not going to let that happen."

She forced a laugh. "Getting your first witness killed probably wouldn't bode so well for your career as a marshal."

"Don't even talk like that."

"Sorry, just trying to lighten the mood a bit with an ill-timed joke."

"Why don't you tell me about why you became a sketch artist? You told me how you did, but why?"

"You really want to know?"

"Yeah."

"I felt like it was a way to use my gift for something positive. I knew I was a talented artist, but drawing pretty things didn't quite feel like enough. Then I felt even more determined once I found faith. God gave me a special talent, and I want to be able to use it."

Back to God again, he thought. But he couldn't blame her. He'd been the one to ask the question. "Your faith is commendable even if I don't adhere to it."

"Why are you so hostile?"

"I'm not hostile," he quickly added.

"You're on the defensive."

"I'm not. It's just that I've seen supposed faith in action, and I have a hard time accepting it."

"Since it obviously makes you uncomfortable, we can talk about something else."

He wasn't uncomfortable, was he? Sydney had a way of reading him, and he was beginning to dislike it. He'd grown to be a man of thought and action, not one of feeling and faith. The only thing he had faith in was himself. Hadn't everyone else in his life failed him in one way or another?

His family life may have looked wonderful on the outside. Two supposedly loving parents, both doctors who were highly respected in their fields. But Max had been just a fashion piece to them. Neither his mother nor his father had really cared about him, and the only time they had had any opinion of him it had been negative.

When he'd chosen to go into law enforcement instead of medical school after college, they had practically disowned him. But he didn't need them or anyone else, for that matter. He'd learned long ago to rely only on himself.

By the time the two of them drove into Pikeville, it was early evening. After they settled into their adjoining hotel rooms at the Pikeville Inn, Max went to Sydney's room to discuss their next steps. He found her pacing back and forth.

"I should tell you something," Sydney said.

"What?" Max asked. He looked over at her. Her lips were pursed and her eyebrows narrowed. He had no idea what she was going to say.

"I didn't bring this up right away because it didn't really seem relevant," Sydney said. "But I've had some time to think it over, and now listening to everything you've said about the FBI and the lack of connection between Kevin and his cousin Lucas, I just need to put it out there."

"What is it?"

Sydney started pacing back and forth again. "Maybe the FBI is right. Maybe this doesn't have anything to do with Lucas trying to protect Kevin."

"Why do you say that?" Max asked.

Sydney glanced away and then made eye contact with him. "Because there's another reason the East River gang could be after me."

THREE

Sydney looked directly at Max. It was time to talk about something she really didn't want to discuss. "I'm sorry I didn't tell you this earlier, but it didn't really occur to me. I was so focused on Kevin and the trial." That wasn't the only reason. She was afraid and ashamed to talk about it. But now she saw she had no choice.

She was about to share a big part of herself with this man. Would he understand? Could she trust him with her painful past?

"What is it?" Max asked.

"It's a long story, but I need to explain it all for it to make sense."

"I'm not going anywhere."

Still she hesitated. "It's not something I normally talk about with anyone, but I feel like you need to know."

"Take your time."

She sat down in one of the hotel chairs, and he took a seat next to her. Hoping she had the strength to reveal her darkest secret to a man she barely knew, she began her story. "I started self-defense training five years ago."

"What happened to make you start?"

She paused and took a deep breath before she answered. "I was dating this guy. Things were going well. But then he began to question my work and become very controlling. He put me down and called what I did a *hobby* that shouldn't interfere with what he expected me to do for him around his apartment. Then when I'd get home late from work, he'd become irate."

He crossed his arms and leaned back. "And that led to worse things happening, right?"

She nodded, fighting off the emotion that came flooding back over her. "One night he'd gone out with his friends. He'd had a few drinks, and when I questioned him about whether he should've driven home he got really angry. I knew he had a temper, but this was the first time I was actually afraid of him."

"I'm worried about what you're going to say next."

"It's exactly what you would expect. He got violent. I had absolutely no way of defending myself." She let out a shaky breath. "But he apologized and I gave him another chance. I chalked it up to a one-time thing."

"And it wasn't," he said softly.

"Definitely not. I lived in fear for months. Some days were fine and perfectly normal. But there were times that were just like the first. Except that each incident got progressively worse. He was verbally and physically abusive." She fought to keep her composure as tears stung her eyes.

He patted her hand. "It's okay, Sydney. Take your time."

"What really changed things for me was not just that he was so awful to me. I thought I could handle that. Really I did. But it all came crashing down on me when he hurt my cat."

"What?"

"I had adopted a stray cat. The cutest little black furry cat you'd ever seen. I named him Bach because I love classical music. He knew how much Bach meant to me. And one day he kicked him so hard, I knew he had to have injured him, and then he put Bach outside the apartment. I literally searched all night until I found him. I was able to get him into a special animal rescue that I worked with. They gave him medical care and thankfully he recovered. But I was devastated that he'd hurt such an innocent animal. That one act of violence against the cat I loved so much was actually what it took to convince me to leave. It was one thing for me to take his abuse, but when he hurt Bach, I knew I'd never be the same."

"What did you do?"

"I got out. Right after I took Bach to the rescue, I ran away the first chance I got. I didn't have anywhere to go, so I ended up driving to a town in the North Georgia mountains. I found a church, and they were able to help me start a new life."

He looked over at her. "Sydney, I don't even know what to say."

"You don't have to say anything." She took a moment to steady herself. "That's when I found faith. I also decided that I would never be a victim again. I started with basic self-defense courses, but that wasn't enough. I saved up my money and got one-on-one training from a former marine who owned a gym. I also started working out to gain more strength. It was one of the best investments I ever made. I stayed in that town for about a year. I volunteered at the animal shelter because I missed Bach so much. But I still couldn't adopt another cat at that point. I had to focus on myself and getting stronger. Make a safe place for myself before becoming responsible for another."

"That makes sense to me."

"I've never let another man into my life after that." And she never would again. She'd made that promise to herself after she got away from the monster. Loneliness was a much better alternative.

Max reached out and gently touched her arm. "You can't let one awful man ruin the rest of your life."

"As you can imagine, the stress of this situation has brought back a lot of those memories, so you have to forgive me if I…can't deal."

"Yes, I understand completely. What you're probably experiencing is a form of post-traumatic stress that has been aggravated. I'm so sorry you're having to go through this, Sydney. If there was anything I could do to make it go away, believe me, I would."

She leaned forward and looked him in the eyes. "I don't want you to think I can't handle myself. Because I can."

"You've already more than proven that to me."

"Thanks, but unfortunately that's not even the real reason I'm telling you this painful story."

His eyes narrowed. "What else is there?"

"My ex." She took a breath, steadied herself. "He had close friends in the East River gang, and after I left I think he got more involved with them. Last I heard he was doing time, but

I haven't kept close tabs on him. I just want to make sure that I never see him again."

"What's his name?"

"Rick Ward." She hated even speaking those words.

"I'll need to run a check on him ASAP. Maybe he saw you in all of the local trial publicity," Max said quietly. "Do you think he is actually a member of the gang?"

"I don't know for sure, but's it's definitely possible. He didn't tell me everything. He was pretty secretive about what he was doing and about his friends. I overheard a conversation one day when a friend of his came to the apartment. They were in the living room watching TV while I was making dinner in the kitchen. They were talking about some other members of East River. At the time I knew it was bad news, but I didn't understand it was actually a violent gang. Although it makes sense now, because it wasn't long after he started hanging around with those friends that he got so violent."

"You did the right thing by telling me all of this, Sydney. But we shouldn't get ahead of ourselves. Let me do some digging and find out if he's still in prison, and whether the FBI has any current intel on his connections to the East River gang."

She swiped at a tear that threatened to fall. She never talked about this to anyone—except to God in her prayers. The only reason she had opened up to this man was because he'd proven that he was willing to put his life on the line for hers. And he deserved to know all of the facts even if it made her uncomfortable to relive the past.

"He'd have to be a big enough player in the gang for East River to take action on his behalf," Max explained. "We can't discount that as a possibility. But either way, East River is involved in the attacks against you. That much I'm sure of."

"I agree, and I felt like I had to say something."

"I'm glad you told me." He knelt down beside her. "You're looking a little pale. Why don't you rest for a few minutes? Then we'll go and get something to eat. Meanwhile, I'll make the phone call to get the ball rolling on the FBI's end."

Max sat across from Sydney in a large booth at the Pikeville Diner, located right next to the inn. It killed Max to see Sydney look so worried. But with each passing minute she impressed him more. Her story of abuse broke his heart, but he had a tremendous amount of respect for her. Max thought men who abused women were the lowest of the low. He wondered how a woman like Sydney could've even met a man like Ward. But it wasn't his business to pry into those types of facts. He had all the relevant information he needed to work his case.

He knew it had taken a lot of courage for her to speak up. Ever since he'd seen her wrestle the gun from the guy at the car, he'd had a feeling that something had caused her to get that self-defense training, but he'd had no idea that it had been something so bad.

What made matters worse was that if the threat to Sydney was purely from her ex-boyfriend, and if there was no connection to Kevin Diaz, then he was worried they might pull the marshals off her. That was one reason he was pushing the Diaz angle. He refused to leave her alone in harm's way. His fallback position with Elena was going to be that regardless of the exact connection, she was a current target because of her testimony. If more than one person had a beef with her, then so be it. In his mind, all roads led back to East River. It was the common thread.

And now he was going to have to break some additional bad news to Sydney. She deserved to know the truth. "I got word back from the FBI."

"And?" she asked with a raised eyebrow.

"Rick Ward was released early from prison for good behavior last month."

Fear flicked through her dark eyes. Then she looked down and back up at him. "It could still be a coincidence."

"Or he could be working on behalf of East River. He gets revenge against you, and it solves the problem of your damaging testimony against Kevin Diaz."

"Assuming he kills me."

"I'm not going to let that happen."

She pushed her plate away, leaving a half-eaten burger.

"If the gang figured out his connection to you, then they could exert pressure on him to go after you. Or vice versa. He uses East River resources to exact his revenge."

"That's true. I didn't see the faces of the shooters at the courthouse. And we didn't see anyone at the first safe house."

"Can you give me his description?"

She gave a weak smile. "I can do better than that." She pulled a small sketchpad out of her bag and went to work.

He watched as her pencil swept with ease over the paper creating a sketch within minutes. She was in her element, but he also wanted to use this as an opportunity to talk more about her work—and his concerns about it.

"This is his face," she said as she turned the drawing toward Max. "He's approximately six feet tall, two hundred pounds. Dark hair with light blue eyes. You can see his other features here. A strong jawline, dimple on the left cheek, a few freckles."

He stared at the face. At first glance, the subject didn't look like a violent man, but Max knew better than to make a judgment based on appearances. Sometimes the people you least suspected were the most violent.

He took a moment more to examine the drawing, but he couldn't deny his inherent skepticism. "Can I ask you something?"

"Yes."

"How can you be so sure that this sketch is accurate? That any sketch you do is accurate?"

Her eyes widened. "Are you questioning my abilities as a sketch artist?"

He shook his head. "Not you specifically. It's just that when I was a rookie in the FBI, I got burned badly by a sketch artist. Turns out we got the wrong guy. The guy who actually committed the crime was able to murder another innocent person. I lost many a night's sleep over that."

She leaned back from the table. "It's an art not a science."

"Exactly. So there's bound to be human error."

"But even from a scientific approach you wouldn't throw out all drawings just because some are flawed. Remember, the sketch artist is only as good as the eyewitness account. And we all know the high rate of error in witness accounts."

"But this sketch." He pointed down to the paper. "This drawing is accurate because you're drawing based on your personal knowledge of him over time. Not just a single account like a witness in a lawsuit for example."

"Yes, that's true. The error rate on a sketch like this is much lower given how well I knew this man—assuming the person drawing has the requisite artistic ability. You can't really compare what I did just now to what would happen normally where I would meet with a witness and then draw based on their factual description."

"That's precisely my point though. I'm sorry if I offended you. It's just something that was on my mind."

"Don't let one bad experience with a sketch artist impact your view of what I do. I take my work and its accuracy very seriously."

He'd obviously hit a nerve. "Like I said, I wasn't trying to question you specifically."

She crossed her arms. "Regardless of what your intent was, you're basically questioning my career. At a time when I'm a key witness in a high-profile case."

She was right. He never should've opened his mouth. "I'm sorry. I wasn't thinking about that."

"It's like you're trying to ice the kicker. Don't forget I still have to testify." She laughed even though he could tell that she wasn't exactly filled with humor.

"Forget I even brought it up. Let's talk about something else." He knew he'd offended her and didn't know if she was going to let it drop.

"How long are we staying in Pikeville?"

"We'll have to play it by ear. I want to see what intel the FBI has on Ward."

The petite waitress with bleached blond hair walked over and pulled their bill out of her notepad. Then she quirked a curious eyebrow. "You two here visiting the town?"

He jumped in, not wanting to put any extra pressure on an already stressed Sydney. "Just passing through for work."

"Ah, well, I hope you enjoyed the food here." She frowned when she saw Sydney's half-eaten burger.

"It was delicious. Just a bit too much." Sydney smiled at her.

The waitress nodded and walked away.

"Let's get back to the hotel," he said. "Try to get some rest. We're going to need it."

Sydney awoke with a start. Darkness surrounded her, and something flashed in her peripheral vision. Where was she? And what was that shuffling noise she heard? Then it came flooding back to her. She was in a hotel room in Pikeville. But she wasn't alone.

Her eyes adjusted to the dark, and she saw a figure in her room. She opened her mouth with an instinctive urge to scream, but the intruder lunged on top of her, silencing her with his hand over her mouth.

"You're coming with me," the man said in a low, menacing voice. The only thing she knew for sure was that the attacker wasn't her ex-boyfriend Rick. But that didn't change her determination to fight him off. No way was she letting him take her out of that hotel room.

He was strong, but she was trained so something like this could never happen again. She refused to be a victim. She was a fighter. Saying a quick prayer for strength, she bit down on his hand as hard as she could.

The intruder yelped and when he loosened

his grip she screamed to alert Max through the unlocked adjoining door. But she wasn't going to wait for Max to come to her rescue. No, she reared back and connected hard with the attacker's jaw with a right uppercut. He stumbled a bit, and she delivered a swift kick to his midsection, forcing him to double over from the impact.

"Sydney!" Max's voice rang out in the darkness.

The intruder ran quickly toward her door, throwing it open and escaping into the night. Then Max came into her room. She could see in the shadows that his gun was drawn.

"He just ran out," she said.

"Stay here." He ran out the door, but she didn't listen to him. She was right behind him.

"There." She pointed toward the parking lot. The man, dressed all in black, was at the edge of the parking lot jumping into a dark colored sedan.

"I can't go after him and leave you by yourself," Max said. "We don't know that he was alone."

"No. You should go. You need to interrogate him."

"It's too risky. I'm sorry. My first priority is always going to be your personal protection. I can't pursue him under the circumstances."

She watched as her attacker disappeared from sight into the darkness.

"Are you all right?"

She shook out her right hand. "Yeah. My hand hurts a bit from punching him, but I'll be fine." She took in a breath of air, realizing that she was breathing hard. "But how did he find me? That's the question we need to answer first."

She walked back into her hotel room, and he was right behind her. She flipped on the light.

"I can tell you're frustrated, and you have every right to be. You were just attacked in the middle of the night. And you're right about how you were found. This location wasn't even in the system. So an electronic system breach wouldn't have provided this information."

He paced back and forth. His dark hair was slightly disheveled from sleep. Then he turned back to face her with his eyes wide. "I need to look through your stuff. Your bag, your purse. Anything you've had on your person since yesterday."

She got what he was saying. "You think someone put some type of tracking device in my stuff?"

He nodded. "It would make a lot of sense, and it would explain all of these breaches."

"But that would also mean someone got close enough to me to put the device in my bag."

"Let me see if I can find anything first."

She handed him her shoulder bag that included her sketch pad. She also gave him her much smaller purse.

"That day at the courthouse. Did you have both of these on you?"

"Yes. My purse was actually in my shoulder bag. I take that bag pretty much everywhere I go, though."

He started with her shoulder bag. It was full of junk. Pencils, pens, some makeup. He unceremoniously dumped out the contents on the hotel-room desk.

She watched as he ran his hands along the lining of her bag. Then he pulled something out.

"This—" he held up a small black chip that looked like a piece of plastic "—is a tracking device. Feels like they used a bit of an adhesive to stick it in the bottom of your bag. You wouldn't notice it unless you were specifically looking for it."

"Wow," she said. "Someone had to have gotten a hold of my bag to get it in the bottom, though. That's disturbing."

"It's actually much easier than you might think. All they had to do was get close enough to you to reach in your bag and quickly adhere the chip inside. More than likely they ran into you—acting like it was purely accidental. But it was all carefully orchestrated."

"It sounds professional. Not just like some random thug could do it."

He nodded. "And it has upper-level East River written all over it." He took a step back. "You know Rick Ward. Do you think he has the ability to climb up the hierarchy of an organization like East River?"

She thought for a moment. "He's definitely not the smartest man I've ever met, but he isn't dumb. He knows how to get what he wants and can be very manipulative. He's also persistent. He won't stop until he has his way by whatever means necessary."

He touched her shoulder. "I hate to do this, Sydney. I know it's the middle of the night, but we need to get out of here."

"What are we going to do with the chip?"

"Leave it here in the hotel room. And then we'll go. We finally have a bit of an advantage. We found the chip, and they don't know that. They'll assume we're here overnight. When the chip doesn't move in the morning, then they'll know we were on to them. But that still gives us a few hours' head start."

"They could be watching us now."

"Yes, that's why I'll also use evasive maneuvers to ensure that we're not being followed. Gather your things and do what you need to do. I want to be on the road in fifteen minutes."

As she prepared to leave, the different scenarios played out in her mind. She was being hunted, but by whom? A professional hit man paid off by a murderer? Or a man she'd thought she loved? She didn't know if she could handle coming face to face with Rick Ward again. A chill shot through her just thinking about those blue eyes. Sweet one minute and menacing the next.

But there was no time for fear right now. They had to hit the road. Her life depended on it.

Max sat behind the wheel fully alert. Even running on only a few hours of sleep, he could feel that his adrenaline had kicked in and he was moving full steam ahead. Sydney must have felt the same way because every time he glanced over at her, she looked wide-awake with her eyes firmly glued to the dark road in front of them.

He couldn't stop the strong need deep within him to protect this woman. But that was all it was. A desire to do his job to the best of his ability. His career was everything to him. At thirty-three he really was in no rush for a serious relationship. He even considered never getting married and having a family. His own family had given him plenty of reasons to roll solo. Yeah, to all the neighbors they may have looked like the perfect family, but his childhood had been far from perfect.

He hadn't met another women quite like Sydney, though. But he had to be realistic. She was definitely not the one for him—assuming someone out there was for him. They were polar opposites on pretty much every issue. Her entire approach to life was guided by emotion and instinct, while his was based on science and logic. She'd even called him hostile to faith. That had seemed a bit much to him at the time, but maybe she was right. His parents hadn't exactly acted as good role models on that front. He preferred to rely on himself and live in a world where he occupied his time with his career. He didn't lack a sense of self-awareness— he knew he had erected walls to make sure he wouldn't get hurt. But that was fine with him.

"Where are we going?" she asked, cutting into his thoughts.

"Elena said to just start driving northwest, but I don't want to stop until we have more distance between us and Pikeville."

"I've been keeping watch out the back," she

said, turning around again to peer out the rear window. "I don't think we've been followed."

"Me, neither."

"Guess that's one positive."

"Hey now. Don't sound so down. That was a big break for us to find that tracker."

"I do thank God for that. But…"

"But what?"

"I really can't describe to you how I feel about Rick." She paused. "And the prospect of seeing him again."

"I won't let him hurt you. And hopefully he has nothing to do with this."

"Maybe not. But I know he would come after me if he could. If he knew where I was, if he had the opportunity. Men like him don't take it very well when a woman leaves them."

"We're going to make sure he doesn't have that opportunity. You have to remember you're not alone now."

"I once was. And those were some dark days. Until I walked into that church and my life changed forever for the better. I know you don't want to hear that, but my faith is all I have. It's what has sustained me when I thought that I might not even want to live."

His heart hurt hearing the emotion dripping from her words. He couldn't help but be moved by what she said. To be moved by her. And to feel that there was a void in his own life from turning away from his faith.

"I don't want your pity," she said quietly.

"Sydney, the last thing in the world I feel for you is pity. You've shown what a strong person you are. You fought that guy off all by yourself. But beyond your physical abilities, you're rock solid emotionally, too. Stronger than a lot of people I know. And a lot of federal agents I've worked with. You can hold your own."

She didn't respond but sat quietly, and he wanted her to believe him. Before he could press his point, his phone rang. He answered and put it on speaker.

"Hey, Max. It's Elena."

"You have something?" Max asked.

"Yes. I have news. Big news."

FOUR

"What is it?" Max asked Elena.

Sydney held her breath, bracing herself for
the worst and waiting on Elena to respond.

"The FBI has apprehended Kevin Diaz,"
Elena reported. "Just as I suspected, his law-
yer argued that there was some misunderstand-
ing on his client's part about what activities he
could still tend to while he was on bail."

"Where is Diaz now?" Max asked.

"While the judge didn't seem as upset as I
would hope, he has revoked his bail and put
him into police custody. The judge is going
to hear arguments about when the trial should
go forward." Elena didn't hesitate as she out-
lined the next steps. "We're going to request
a meeting with the judge to discuss the security situation for Ms. Berry. I already spoke
to the prosecutor. She feels like there are too
many variables to directly attribute the attacks
on Ms. Berry to Kevin Diaz since we can't

present direct evidence of a tie between Diaz and his cousin Lucas Jones. She wants to try to spin the attacks as some other dispute that Ms. Berry has with East River. I, of course, didn't bring up Ward at this juncture, as that would've only added more fuel to her fire. So the bottom line is that the prosecutor is going to push for an immediate resumption of trial. Her main concern is getting Diaz convicted of first-degree murder."

"That's ridiculous," Max said.

"Her exact quote was, 'You do your job and I'll do mine.' She thinks we can keep Ms. Berry safe."

Max slammed his hand on the dashboard. "That's beside the point. The point is that she is testifying for the state as their expert witness. And in doing so she is putting her life in jeopardy."

"The prosecutor doesn't see it that way," Elena replied. "But she's offering to push a request for witness protection after Ms. Berry's testimony."

"Great," Sydney said. She couldn't control her sarcasm.

"In the prosecutor's mind it's a solution for everyone."

Sydney scoffed. "I love how she's making life-changing decisions for me. What if I don't want to go into witness protection? What if I want to keep doing what I'm doing with my work? How could I? I'd never be able to testify at trials anymore."

"I understand your concerns," Elena said. "But I'd urge you not to think about the prosecutor's agenda and instead think about what is best for you. Especially now that Ward is back on the street. You would never be able to go in to witness protection solely from a threat he posed because you have to be a testifying state's witness. This is an opportunity to get away from him for good. To truly start a new life. A life in which he'll never find you because Sydney Berry will no longer exist. You're never going to get this opportunity again."

Sydney thought about that for a minute. "This is a lot to take in. I need to think about it."

"Sure," Elena said. "I'll let you two know what decisions come out of the discussions with the court. Drive safely."

Max ended the call, and Sydney looked out the window as the first signs of sunrise broke into the sky.

"Say something," he said.

Keeping her eyes on the sky, she replied quietly, "I'm glad Kevin Diaz is now in custody. I think I should testify again as soon as possible.

He shouldn't be able to avoid justice." Her voice grew stronger as she continued. "But I really don't want to give up my life—a life I literally fought for. It means a lot to me to be able to be who I am, as I am."

"Sydney, it's a huge decision. You need to seriously examine your options. And while I want nothing more than to be able to ensure your complete safety, witness protection is the easiest way. But it's not the only way, and you shouldn't be forced to sacrifice everything you love in the career that you've built from the ground up. I get that."

As she looked at him, she realized that he actually understood what she was saying. This man whom she'd only known for a few short days seemed to get her more than any other person ever had. She couldn't explain it. They were so different. Had God brought this man into her life for a purpose?

"I appreciate you saying all of that." She hadn't gotten close to a man since her ex-boyfriend and had no plan to in the future. Trust didn't come easy to her, but Max was earning her trust by continuing to put it all on the line for her. But trusting in him to help protect her was as far as she would let it go.

"But I wouldn't be doing my job if I didn't say that this isn't just about the testimony and the security at trial. If your ex-boyfriend is a player with East River, then you could always be a target. And that's not a good way to live, either."

"There's no good solution. I'm going to be looking over my shoulder forever."

Max had a sinking feeling in the pit of his stomach. He knew it wouldn't be long before he was driving Sydney back to the courthouse in downtown Atlanta.

They'd checked into adjoining rooms in a small hotel in Baymont, Alabama, and taken a nap for a few hours—until his sleep was interrupted by a call from Elena. The judge was prepared to move forward with the trial starting tomorrow, which included testimony from Sydney, if she so chose. While the judge had ordered additional courthouse security, Max felt like a target would be plastered on her back.

He decided to check in with Davies and see if he had gotten any further information from the FBI. He would've preferred to call his FBI contacts directly, but Davies was working with the FBI sources while Max focused on Sydney's security.

"Davies, you got anything?"

"Rick Ward did have strong affiliations with East River, but no one has any insight on any current activities. My guess is that Ward is long gone by now. The FBI is more focused on the link between Diaz and Lucas Jones."

"Got it."

"Elena just gave me word that you'll be bringing our witness back here to testify. Once you get in the vicinity, I'm going to be with you, too. We're taking every precaution."

"I don't like it, but I know Sydney's going to want to testify."

"You're sure of it?" Davies asked.

"I haven't told her of the trial resuming yet, but I already know what her answer is going to be."

"Then we'll do our job. Let me know when you get close."

Max hung up the phone and dreaded the conversation he needed to have with Sydney. It was as he'd told Davies. Sydney was going to insist on testifying. On doing her job. He admired the fact that she wouldn't back down, even though he wanted so badly to whisk her away and keep her safe. His feelings for Sydney went beyond his job description. He was starting to care about her as a person. He hadn't even realized he was capable of feeling emotions anymore, and it was comforting and unsettling at the same time.

No matter what, he had to remain professional and keep the proper distance. Sydney was fighting to maintain control over her life, and he had a job to do.

Taking a breath, he walked over to the adjoining hotel-room door and knocked. It wasn't long before the door opened. Her hair had fallen partially out of a bun, and she had a faint pillow line on the side of her face. He was glad to see that she'd gotten a little rest.

"Sorry to wake you, but I've got updates."

"What?" Her brown eyes widened.

"The judge has ordered the trial to resume tomorrow. Assuming you still want to testify, you will do so in the morning. The judge has ordered extra courthouse security, and Davies will be assisting me with your personal security. There will be additional US Marshal presence all around the courthouse."

She didn't immediately respond. Her eyes looked down and then met his. "You know I'm going to testify, right?"

He nodded. "I assumed that's what you would say."

She took a step closer to him and placed her hand on his shoulder. "I appreciate everything you've done for me to keep me safe, but I have to do this. I think you can understand that."

He took her hand from his shoulder and

held it tightly in his. "And I will continue to do everything in my power to keep you safe."

"I know that, Max. You may not believe this, but I know there's a greater plan at work. I have to believe that."

"I respect your feelings even if I don't share them."

She gripped his hands even more tightly. "I'm not afraid. Not of this. And I know you'll be there with me every step of the way."

She didn't immediately let go of his hands. And when she did he felt saddened by the loss of connection to her.

"When do we go back to Atlanta?" she asked.

"Tonight."

"Okay."

"And one more thing. Davies said the FBI hasn't found anything current on Ward and his ties to East River, even though there were definite affiliations in the past. He thinks Ward's probably out of the picture."

"I hope so." She paused. "But there's no way that I'm letting down my guard."

"As you shouldn't. There's too much going on for you to do that."

"I'm ready to get this over with."

Sydney hadn't slept much last night in the Atlanta hotel room. She was on edge and running on the pure anticipation of testifying at the trial. Now only a few miles away from the courthouse, Max was on the phone with Davies coordinating her security.

Testifying was important to her. It was one thing she could do that was in her control. What she couldn't control were the threats—or the ramifications of her testimony.

"We're stopping and Davies will be over here in a minute." Max pulled the car into a parking lot a good ways from the courthouse. "We'll both take you inside with the assistance of the other marshals working security. And there's a team securing the perimeter, as well."

She looked over at him and could almost feel the tension radiating off his body. "If it's so secure, why are you gripping the wheel so tightly?"

He shook his head. "I think you know my opinion, Sydney. I want you as far away from here as possible."

"It's going to be all right." She closed her eyes for a moment.

"Are you praying?" he asked.

"Yes."

The air thickened in anticipation. But nothing was going to make her change her decision to testify against Diaz.

"Davies is here," Max said.

She was a bit relieved to see her additional security pulling up in a black sedan. The rising tension between her and Max was making her nervous.

"Stay in the car for a second while I talk to him," Max ordered.

Not waiting for her to argue, he opened the door and stepped out. But it wasn't long before he returned and Davies slid into the backseat.

"Not to worry," Davies told her. "We're going to get you in and out of the courthouse today with no problem." He smiled.

Davies was obviously feeling more confident than Max as they drove toward the courthouse.

"We're parking around the back. There's more security waiting there for us. They know we're coming," Max said.

Her heartbeat sped up when the car stopped. She saw the additional marshals all in suits awaiting their arrival. She was as safe as she could possibly be, she told herself. Just look at all the extra security.

"It's time," Max said.

Davies got out of the car and opened her door, ushering her out. He was on her right and Max was on her left, while the throng of marshals provided cover as they entered a back door to the courthouse.

"You're going to be in one of the conference

rooms with the two of us until they're ready for you to testify. Additional security will be surrounding the courthouse. No one is getting in without being screened."

She nodded as they guided her through the courthouse corridor. Max opened the door to the conference room and looked around, then he motioned her and Davies in. The room held nothing but a single table and a few chairs.

"So we'll have to wait a few minutes, but it was better to get you in here and settled," Max said. "Once the judge brings in the jury, then we'll get you in the courtroom for your testimony."

Davies spoke to the marshal outside the door and then closed it. "Sorry that things have been so hectic for you, Sydney. I'm guessing Max told you, but no one in the FBI gang unit has been able to come up with any recent connections between Ward and East River. Maybe that can bring you a small measure of comfort."

"It does, thank you. I'd rather take my chances with East River without Rick Ward involved." She took a seat and drummed her fingers on the table. Nothing to do now but wait. At least she was safely in the courthouse. The hardest part was over. "Where's Elena?"

"She running point on the general courthouse security," Davies said.

They sat in silence for a few minutes while

she tried to get back into expert witness mode. After all, that was why she was there. To testify in a murder trial. To provide evidence to assist the jury in determining the guilt of Kevin Diaz—something she had no doubt about, even if Max had inadvertently questioned the reliability of her work.

Her thoughts were interrupted by a blaring alarm. "What's that?" she asked, trying to cover her ears. The sound was almost at a deafening pitch pulsing through body.

Davies held a hand to his ear, obviously getting information from an earpiece. "It's a bomb threat. We've got to move now." He pushed his earpiece again. "We're moving the witness. Everyone stick to code-red protocol." Then he tapped his earpiece.

"Wait," Max said. He stood protectively beside her. "Think about it," he yelled over the sound of the alarm. "A bomb makes absolutely no sense. Kevin Diaz is in the courthouse. He wouldn't want to die. This would be an act of suicide on his part."

"We don't have a choice, Max. This could be an unrelated threat. There is specific procedure for this. I know you're new on the job, but as a marshal we don't break protocol."

"You've got to think outside of the box sometimes when facts dictate it," Max said.

"In the event of a bomb threat, we evacuate the witness. Period." Davies pulled Sydney up from the chair and walked toward the door.

Max blocked their path. "No. It's a trap to draw her out. I can feel it."

"We don't operate by intuition," Davies snapped.

The two men stood facing each other, neither wanting to back down. What was going to happen? The alarm kept sounding, and she could hear yells and screams from the corridor.

"I'm not letting you take her out of here." Max grabbed Davies's arm.

"You're going to get fired for this," Davies said, shaking free of Max's grip. "Your career will be over."

"Better to get fired than to get my witness killed." He took another step toward Davies. "You're going to have to get through me before you can take her out of here. And I don't think you're prepared to do that."

"Enough," Sydney said. "I should get a say in this."

"That's not how it works," Davies replied. He tried to push Max aside and reached for the door. "She's coming with me."

"No," Max said, not backing down.

Then Davies wrapped his arm around her neck, squeezing tightly. She gasped for air.

What in the world was he doing? He was hurting her.

"I didn't want to have to do this, but you're forcing my hand." His left arm was squeezing her neck, choking off her air supply and the other hand held his gun. "Sydney is coming with me. And you're going to back off before something bad happens to your witness."

Sydney tried to take a breath but her air was being cut off. She watched the recognition flash through Max's eyes as the truth hit her squarely, too.

"You're working for East River," Max said.

"I'll kill her right here if you don't step aside now," Davies commanded. "Handcuff yourself to the leg of the desk."

What was Max going to do now? She prayed for God to help save her from this man.

Max moved slowly back toward the desk, his hands up in the air. "I'm doing what you say. Just don't hurt her."

Thankfully, she felt Davies's grip loosen around her neck. She focused her eyes on Max. She couldn't believe that he would let the rogue marshal take her. Did he have a plan?

Max glanced down quickly at the weapon at his side. That was all she needed to see. He was going to take a shot. She just had to be ready. She gave him the tiniest of nods.

And then Max made the move for his gun, and she flung herself quickly to the floor, hitting it hard.

The gunshot hit Davies in the shoulder. He howled and fell to the ground beside her.

Max ran to her and grabbed her up off the ground. "We've got to move. I don't know how far the marshals have been compromised."

Because of the bomb evacuation, the halls were already empty.

"Stay as close as you can to me." He pulled her into him as they ran down the corridor toward the back door. "Whatever happens, don't stop running. Don't stop for anyone."

Her mind flooded with thoughts of Davies's stinging betrayal. As a US Marshal, he was supposed to have protected her. Instead he'd sold her out to East River.

Max pushed through the back exit of the courthouse that they had come in from and the scene was mass chaos. People running and screaming.

"Agent Preston," a female voice rang out. It had to be Elena. But Max didn't show any sign of stopping as he pressed forward.

"Don't look back. Keep running," Max told her.

Elena's voice sounded again, but they got lost in the crowd of people running away from the courthouse. When they reached his car he ordered her to get in.

They sped away before she could even buckle up.

"We've got to get another car, and we're dumping our burner cells that Elena got us." His eyes scanned the road.

"You don't really think she's working with Davies, do you?" she asked.

"I hope not, but we can't take that risk. There's only one person I know for certain that I can trust. A former FBI colleague. I've got to get another burner phone and contact him. But first we've got to get out of here."

She felt the car accelerate even faster as he made his way quickly to the highway. "I have a feeling this isn't exactly standard operating procedure for the US Marshals."

"Well, it's not every day that one of our own is a traitor, either. East River must have something big on him. Or they're just offering him a ton of money and he couldn't resist."

"He would've killed me." The realization hit home and chills shot down her arms.

"Yes, or handed you over to East River for them to do it." He paused. "But what's important is that you're out of there. It didn't happen."

"What do you think his plan was?"

"To take you out in the evacuation chaos and

then hand you off or disappear with you. He didn't count on me challenging him. That threw a wrench into everything because he needed the crowd to cover his moves."

"But you knew something was off."

"Bombs don't make sense when the perpetrator would also be killed. Unless it was a suicide mission, and I know that's not how Kevin Diaz operates. He wouldn't die by his own hand. His ego is far too big for that."

"I guess Davies was willing to sacrifice his job."

"He probably thought he could do it without getting caught. Claim that he got ambushed and you got taken. Then he'd still be working on the inside. That would be the perfect plan for him and for East River."

"But one that you foiled."

"We foiled. He miscalculated trying to play it safe by not taking me out. He probably assumed killing me might solve one problem but just create another." For the first time he glanced her way, and he smiled. "You were great. Kept your cool and reacted quickly to my cues."

"I have to admit for a brief second I wondered if you were going to cuff yourself to that desk and let me walk out of there with him."

"And what changed your mind?"

"I know we haven't known each other long, but in that time I feel like I've grown to understand you. You made the calculated risk to act because if you hadn't, you knew I'd be dead if Davies took me. Thank you for taking care of me."

He glanced over at her again, and she felt the warmth emanating from his eyes.

This man was not only her protector. He was becoming a friend. But that was all she would ever let him be.

FIVE

Max had told Sydney there was only one person he knew he could trust. And that was Brian Jenkins, the man standing before her now in a house outside the perimeter of Atlanta. Brian had picked them up at a gas station where they'd abandoned their car.

"You can stay here as long as you need," Brian said.

The tall, blond FBI agent stood across from her. He had a formidable presence and muscular build, but kind brown eyes. She felt especially distrustful of anyone new right now, but if Max believed in this man, then that was good enough for her.

"Thanks for letting us use this house," Max said. "I don't know how long we'll be able to stay, but we needed something safe for the immediate future."

"Can you give me the full rundown now?"

Brian asked. "Let's go sit in the kitchen. I'll get some coffee going."

They walked into the spacious and bright kitchen decorated in a pale yellow. Brian looked over at Sydney as he started the coffee. "I know it doesn't look like a bachelor pad in here. My late wife decorated it."

"I'm so sorry," she said. She could still see the pain in his eyes.

"Thank you. It's been three years, but after she passed away I just couldn't live here anymore, so I got a small condo in the city. I couldn't bear to sell the place, and I come back from time to time." He paused. "But don't worry. No one will look for you here."

"I really appreciate your help." She took a seat at the kitchen table across from Max.

"So tell me what's going on," Brian said as he sat down.

Max proceeded to give him a brief summary minus the Ward angle of what happened up until the encounter with Davies in the courthouse. He didn't want to get into Ward issues at this point and thought it better to focus on the current problem with Davies.

"We've got a dirty US marshal. A guy named Phillip Davies that I thought was one of the good guys. I shot him. Not life threatening or anything. He tried to use a fake bomb threat to kidnap Sydney, or at least that's my theory.

"The problem is that now I'm not sure who I can trust on the inside of the marshals. And for all we know, Diaz told them that I went rogue and kidnapped Sydney. Also, Davies claimed he was working with the FBI on various things, but now I don't know if that was all a lie."

Brian nodded. "I'll try to use my sources to figure out what is going on." He stood and poured coffee into a cup. He handed the first one to her along with the sugar bowl. "I've got powdered cream in the cabinet if you want some. Sorry, I don't have fresh. I don't keep a lot of perishables here."

"I just take sugar," she said.

"And I'm good with black," Max said. "If the marshals believe Davies's story, then we're really in trouble. We'll have to avoid them and the East River gang until the truth comes out. And the problem is that I fled the scene with the witness. Because he's the seasoned marshal it would be logical for them to take his side. Not to mention the fact that I did shoot him."

Brian leaned forward in his chair. "You're right, though. You can't trust the marshals. You don't know how far the corruption has spread. And even if it is isolated, Davies will have the upper hand since he will use his injury to prove his story. And as long as they believe him, he's still in play for East River."

"Exactly. We're going to need your help getting a car," he told his friend.

"No problem. I'll get you a rental sent over. I've got a relationship with one of the local dealers. He always hooks me up, no questions asked."

"I hate to do this to you, but you can't tell any of the other agents in the gang unit about this right now. We can't take the risk that other agents have been compromised by East River."

"I understand. You've got my word on that."

"I guess this means I won't be testifying any time soon," she said softly after she sipped her coffee.

Max looked up at her. "I know you really want to, but given the circumstances that just won't be possible. And after what happened today, the judge may even issue a continuance to get the security situation stabilized."

"But you don't really think Elena could be in on this," she said. "Do you?"

"Who's Elena?" Brian asked.

"My boss. Elena Sanchez." He let out a breath. "With her integrity I can't see her doing something like this. But I can't be blind to dangerous scenarios even if they are remote. I know you like her, Sydney. In the end I hope my initial instincts—and yours—will prove to be right, but in the meantime we're off the grid."

"Good call," Brian said. "The plan will be for you to stay here until you feel like you have to move. I've got plenty of nonperishables, but I can bring over some fresh groceries, too. And I'll get you that rental."

"Great," Max said. "But I don't think we will be here too long, and we can just make do with whatever food you have."

"You do realize that if Davies has convinced the marshals you're the bad guy and have kidnapped the witness, there will be an all-out manhunt for you."

"Which is why I understand how much of a risk you're taking by helping us."

"You saved my life, Max. I know that you're only trying to do what's best to protect Sydney. I'm here for whatever you need."

Max stood up and gave Brian a strong pat on the back. "I appreciate it, man."

"I'm going to get going," Brian said as he rose. "I'll do some recon and get you that car. I'll be back."

Brian walked out of the house leaving the two of them sitting in silence. Sydney didn't know what to say, but Max reached out across the table and touched her arm.

"I've got your back, Sydney. I don't want you to have any doubts about that."

"I don't have any. Not about you."

He stood up and walked over to her, taking her hand as she got out of the chair. "And you certainly shouldn't have any self-doubt. You've been handling everything better than most people would in this position."

Hearing him say that meant a lot to her. She'd struggled all these years to gain strength—not just on the outside but on the inside, too. She looked into his big green eyes and felt a pull toward this man. Unlike anything she felt before. Yes, he was undoubtedly handsome, but that wasn't it. There was a growing connection between them.

"What's wrong?" he asked.

"Nothing. I think everything is finally hitting me." Which was true. There was no time to analyze her feelings toward Max. She needed to focus all of her energy on staying safe and fighting off the threats.

Max tried to stay focused on the mission as he drank his morning coffee. Even in the light of day things didn't look any better, though they'd made it through the night safely.

He paced the kitchen as he thought. Sydney hadn't emerged from her room yet. He knew she had to be exhausted—both mentally and physically.

He worried about her safety—and about her as a person. They both had come to this point in their lives with a lot of baggage. His had to do with his family and how he'd been raised. Hers hinged on her awful experience with Ward. Thinking about Ward made him sick to his stomach. What he wouldn't give to have a few minutes alone with that man.

A loud knock at the front door startled him and he almost spilled his coffee. Brian wouldn't have knocked like that. He grabbed his gun from the holster and walked to the door.

He looked through the peephole. Elena? How had she found them?

"I know you're in there, Max. I need to talk to you now. I'm here alone."

He needed to make sure Sydney was safe. For all he knew, Elena could have the place surrounded. He quickly ran into the living room and looked outside through the curtain. Then he jogged to the back of the house and peered through the window. Nothing.

Would Elena have come alone?

He went back to the front door. "I'm letting you in, Elena, but I've got my weapon pulled."

"That won't be necessary. Once I explain

everything, you'll understand. I know you're trying to keep Sydney safe."

At that point he had to make a quick judgment call. He slowly opened the front door, but he had his gun drawn. There was no question he would shoot to protect Sydney.

Elena walked in slowly with her hands up. "I'm armed but my gun is in the holster. I have no intention of using it, and I hope you don't plan to use yours, either."

He motioned for her to walk farther into the house, but he kept his gun aimed at her.

"What's going on?" Sydney's voice rang out from the upstairs area.

"Ms. Berry, I assume you're here of your own free will?" Elena called out.

"Of course. Davies was the one who tried to kidnap me."

"Sydney, please stay up there for a few minutes while I talk to Elena."

She didn't argue and he heard her footsteps as she walked back toward her room.

Max turned to Elena. "How did you find me?"

"I figured given what happened with Davies you wouldn't trust anyone at the marshals. I remembered that you and I had a conversation during the interview process when you mentioned someone with the last name Jenkins. But don't worry. I operated completely off book in conducting my search, and I ensured that no one could've followed me here."

She was spot on in her analysis about his distrust of the marshals that it was almost scary. "So you say you believe that I'm protecting Sydney. Where is Davies?"

"It's complicated," she said.

"Why do I have the feeling that I'm not going to like anything you have to say from here on out?"

"Why don't we sit down?"

He nodded and motioned toward the kitchen where she took a seat. He still kept his gun out in case he needed it. "Give me your weapon."

"Are you serious?" she asked.

"Yes. I can't trust you right now."

She crossed her arms. "You know I can't do that."

"I'm a fellow marshal, so you certainly can."

Reluctantly, Elena placed the gun on the table and slid it to the far end. "Happy? I can't get to it there. Not before you'd shoot me, anyway."

He sat down across from her. "Tell me what's going on," he said. "Because I can see that there's something I'm missing."

Elena sat up straighter in her chair. "I've had my suspicions about Davies for some time now."

"What? What do you mean *suspicions*?" His

mind raced with the implications of what she was saying.

"I didn't have any proof. Nothing actionable that I could take all the way up the chain of command. But I had noticed some odd behavior patterns. A few things seemed off with him. And then one night I saw him outside a downtown hotel talking with a man that I believe conducts business for East River. Davies didn't see me, and I never confronted him about it."

"Back up." He put his hand up in the air. "You believed that Davies was involved with East River and you entrusted a witness to him?"

"No," she said loudly. "I entrusted the witness to you, Max. Specifically for that reason. I thought that him being tangentially involved in the case would let me know whether there really was something to his actions or not. But I never would've given Sydney's security detail completely over to him. At the time it seemed like a prudent plan."

He pounded his fist on the table. "And in the process you almost got Sydney killed."

"I realize that and I'm fully prepared to hand in my resignation." She paused. "But only after this assignment is over." Her dark eyes were filled with determination.

"So where is Davies now?"

"In the hospital. You got him good in the

shoulder. Not life threatening or anything but there is some damage. He'll probably need some physical therapy to get the full range of motion back."

"He was trying to kidnap Sydney. I had no choice but to take the shot."

She frowned. "I understand that. And, Max, I never dreamed that Davies would actually take offensive action and try to kidnap her. Yeah, I thought maybe he was taking some money from East River for intel, or maybe he got caught up in the drug business. But never did I think anything like what happened would go down."

"The entire bomb threat was a ruse to facilitate his escape with her," he said. "Davies needs to be interrogated as soon as possible."

"Right, but let's take a step back for a moment, though. I think it actually works for us if we keep Davies in play. We've come this far."

"We'll need to discuss how to handle Davies. But you should've told me, Elena." He let out a breath. "I know you're my supervisor, but I had an absolute right to know something like this. How can I ever trust you again?"

She looked down. "I've made a series of bad decisions, and I'm going to have to live with that and accept the consequences."

"I understand what you did," Sydney said.

Max looked up and saw Sydney walk into the kitchen.

"I've heard enough of the conversation," Sydney said. "I don't hold any of this against you, Elena."

"Maybe you should," Max said. "She put your life at risk by running an unsanctioned operation without letting your personal security detail know anything about it." He was trying to stay calm, but seeing how Elena and Sydney were handling this was driving him crazy. Even though Elena was his boss, she had overstepped the proper boundaries and been completely reckless.

"He's right, Sydney. I've failed you, but I want to ensure that nothing else happens to you. I want to fix this."

"If you really mean that, then Davies should be taken into custody right now. He should be in the hospital in handcuffs," Max said.

"Max, you're upset with me and I get that. But you need to think about the bigger picture. If we act now, that would only take out Davies. What if East River has a further reach than just him? Once he knows he's made, then it's all over. East River won't use him anymore. We can't lose this opportunity because the lives of other witnesses are also at stake. The entire integrity of the US Marshals is on the line."

"She's right," Sydney said. "This is bigger than just me. If the East River gang has infiltrated the marshals, then something has to be done."

"The likelihood is that Davies is a lone wolf working for East River," Max said.

"I agree, but you know as well as I do that we can't just assume that."

"Hypothetically speaking, if I did decide to go along with you on this, what exactly is your plan?" Max asked.

"I don't have a plan yet," Elena said. "But I do think that it would be too shortsighted to take Davies out of the picture now. He could be of great use to us."

"I'd want to hear some more concrete ideas."

"I understand. You need to know that I wouldn't do anything to put Sydney in danger."

"You got that right. You've already put Sydney at far too much risk," Max said. He knew he was out of line talking to his boss like that, but he couldn't help himself. Everything had changed.

Elena cast her eyes down. "I'm sorry about that, Max. But right now we've got to focus on the task at hand."

"What did you discuss with Davies?" Max asked.

She looked up at him. "He gave me his version

of events, which I pretended to wholly accept. I told him that I would make sure that you were found and dealt with. And that the witness was recovered."

"And the murder trial?"

"The judge granted a continuance for now. Kevin Diaz will just have to wait in jail. Unless his lawyers pull some strings to get his bail reinstated. Which with his bankroll is totally possible. Regardless, though, the court is going to want some time to investigate the security situation. So even if he gets put back on the trial calendar, I'm sure it will take at least a few days."

"You can't tell anyone that we're here," Max said.

"I realize that. There are significant marshal resources dedicated to finding you and Sydney. I'm going to go now, but I'll be in contact soon." She stood up and went to retrieve her gun from the end of the table, but stopped and looked at Max. When he nodded, she picked up the weapon and holstered it.

Max followed Elena to the door and locked it behind her. Then he turned around and Sydney stood in front of him.

"What're you thinking?" Sydney asked.

"That I don't like how you were used. It makes me question Elena's judgment."

"Do you believe her?"

"I want to, but I'm still a bit skeptical."

"She could've done something while she was here if that was her game plan."

"That's part of the problem. I don't know what her plan is. I haven't known her that long, but she's always been very by the book. Pragmatic, logical and conservative with her choices."

"And this isn't."

"No way."

"But if she suspected Davies, then what else was she supposed to do? She did the right thing by coming over here now and explaining everything."

He walked to her. "Elena should've let me know in the beginning that she suspected Davies. I needed to know that information."

She grabbed his hands. "I trust you. I know we're going to get through this."

The way she looked at him made his breath catch. He was responsible for her safety. Was he up to the task? A moment of self-doubt crept in. What if he failed her?

"What is it?" she asked.

"You have a lot of faith in me."

"You've earned it. You've been nothing but good to me. You've saved my life multiple times. Why should I doubt you?"

He smiled as her words warmed his heart. He realized they were still holding hands. And he wanted more than anything to wrap his arms around her. To protect her.

But he also couldn't deny his feelings that were building for her. He dropped her hands when he heard the door open as Brian walked back inside.

"I've got your car," Brian said. "My buddy from the rental company came through. He followed me over to drop it off." Brian handed him the keys.

Max took the keys and pocketed them. "We had a visitor while you were gone," he said.

"Who? What happened?"

Max filled him in on Elena's visit as Sydney sat by quietly, no doubt taking in whatever details she might have missed. "Ultimately, she's hoping to get some proof of Davies's guilt," he concluded.

"Wow." Brian ran a hand through his hair. "That's a risky move."

"Tell me about it."

"And you had no clue what was happening?"

Max shook his head. "None. She left me completely in the dark."

"Are you sure that she's not in on it?"

Max shot a glance at Sydney before he answered. "I'm not positive," he told Brian. "But she figured out our location and didn't bring backup. If she was in on it and really wanted us, she could've ambushed us with marshals or East River hit men."

"That's a good point. Do you think you should leave?" Brian asked.

"I'm debating it."

"Well, I checked and the marshals do have an APB out for you. They are calling it a kidnapping at this time and saying you're armed and dangerous."

"Oh, no," Sydney said.

Max turned to her. "Given the circumstances, that was to be expected."

Brian agreed. "You know you can stay as long as you want to. But I think it'd be a good idea to get out of the Atlanta area."

"He's right," Sydney said.

"But if we're on the run we're subject to getting pulled over and apprehended," Max objected,

"Your call, man," Brian said. "Whatever I can do, just let me know."

"Any gang chatter about all of this?"

"Radio silence," Brian replied. "I think they know we're on to them and looking to crack down."

"We need evidence to link Kevin Diaz to his cousin Lucas Jones. And I'll need your help."

Brian nodded. "What do you have in mind, Max?"

"An undercover operation."

SIX

Sydney heard the words *undercover operation* and her pulse quickened. Before she could ask any questions, Brian was jumping in.

"I don't like where this is going. You can't go into the East River gang undercover, Max. They obviously know who you are by now. You'd be asking to get yourself killed."

"Believe me. I understand that. Not to mention it's my duty to protect Sydney."

"Then what are you talking about?" Sydney asked.

"For this to work, Brian would actually be the one going undercover."

"Whoa." Brian took a step backward.

Sydney was taken by surprise, too. She never expected that Max would get his friend that far involved.

"I have been thinking it through," Max said.

"This would be an unsanctioned operation," Brian said. "The FBI won't approve this."

"I know I'm asking a lot of you, and I wouldn't ask unless I had no other option. But you have to realize that we're doing the right thing. Once we have hard evidence tying Kevin and Lucas together, then we'll present that to the FBI. Until we have that, we don't have enough to get the FBI to investigate the US Marshals."

Brian let out a breath.

Sydney reached out and touched Brian's arm. "You don't have to do this, Brian. We can figure out something else. There's no need to risk your life and your career."

He smiled at her. "I know. But Max makes a great point. This is a bigger issue that goes to the core of the US Marshals. I can't just stand by if there's something I could do to make sure that innocent people like you are kept safe when they entrust themselves to the government for protection."

"So here's what I was thinking," Max began. Then he stopped. "Let's sit down at the kitchen table first."

Sydney followed the men into the kitchen and took a seat at the table beside Max. Brian sat across from him.

"I'm listening," Brian said.

"So." Max leaned back and crossed his arms.

"I'm going to be upfront with you. This is risky."

"Just spit it out," Sydney heard herself say before she could stop it.

Max sent a faint smile in her direction and then looked back at Brian. "You befriend Lucas Jones."

Brian laughed. "And how exactly do I go about doing that?"

"By posing as a very wealthy investor looking to expand his ties to dirty businesses."

Brian raised an eyebrow but didn't say anything.

Sydney had questions. "Why would Lucas Jones believe that Brian would want in on his businesses?"

"The East River gang is called a gang, but it's much more than that. It's a complex organized crime racket that could always use an additional influx of cash. Brian will offer money, but he'll want things in return." Max paused. "For one, a hefty return on his investment. A money-making venture. But he'll also want information on his competition. His competition including the likes of Kevin Diaz."

Could it work? she asked herself. It might, but was it worth the risk? She turned to Brian. "If Lucas Jones finds out you're an FBI agent, he'll kill you."

Brian nodded. "I won't let that happen."

"But you can't be sure," she said.

"Brian's a professional, Sydney. This is what he does for a living," Max said. "I've been undercover with him before. He's one of the best there is."

"We don't have a lot of time to waste." Brian stood. "If you're serious about this, I need to start working on my cover. I'm not going in with a wire. They'll most definitely check me out. I can't risk it."

"You know that I'm going to be your backup," Max said.

"It's too dangerous. You need to focus on protecting Sydney."

Max shook his head. "We won't get too close. But I'm not going to leave you totally vulnerable. Especially for the first meeting."

"I need to get going. Depending on how much I can get done, we can figure out if I can try to do the meet up with Lucas tomorrow. I know his normal hangouts."

Max rose from his chair and gave Brian a hefty pat on the back. "Thanks, man."

Brian nodded toward Sydney and walked out.

"I can see your mind racing," Max said as he turned to Sydney.

She stood up. "This is far too dangerous, sending him in there like that to face Jones and his East River thugs."

"He'll be fine. It's not his first undercover job." He walked over to her. "This is our best shot at getting the evidence to tie Diaz to Jones. We have no other choice. We have to start being proactive instead of reactive."

"I'm assuming you're not going to say anything to Elena about this?"

"Absolutely not. I think she's on our side, but I'm not willing to risk Brian's life on that assumption."

"What about your own safety?"

He grabbed her hands, sending a shiver down her arms.

"Don't worry about me," he said softly. "My job is to worry about you."

"I can't help but worry." She took a deep breath as Max took a step closer to her.

Then Max's phone buzzed—and the moment ended almost before it began.

Max was playing with fire.

If his phone hadn't rung the night before, he had been very close to wrapping his arms around Sydney. Too close. Even though his brain told him it was an absolutely awful idea, his heart was saying otherwise. He couldn't handle these emotions that were completely foreign to him.

All day he'd tried to put any thought of being more than friends with Sydney out of his mind. Time had passed slowly as he'd done his best to keep his distance from her. The house was large enough for that not to be a big deal.

Now he was on edge as he waited for Brian to return to the house. Brian had been cryptic over the phone, but things sounded as though they were a go for the undercover operation.

"Hey." Sydney walked into the kitchen with a smile that punched him in the gut. He took a deep breath and focused on the case.

"Brian is on his way. I think we'll probably be moving on the operation tonight."

Her brown eyes widened. "What will you need me to do?"

"We'll figure that out once Brian gets here. But I can guarantee I'm not going to do anything to put you in the line of fire."

She placed one hand on her hip. "I'm not so fragile, you know."

"Believe me, you've shown yourself to be anything but fragile. But these guys are out for blood. *Your* blood specifically, and I have to make sure that they don't get close enough to spill any."

He heard the door open signaling Brian's arrival.

"Hey, Sydney." Brian smiled at her as he walked into the kitchen.

"Where do we stand?" Max asked.

Brian took a seat and motioned for them to do the same. "We have a confidential informant who works at the bank where some of the East River money is being funneled. The CI is going to be meeting with Lucas tonight after hours to discuss some money flow issues. The CI won't know that I'm FBI, but I'll still be able to use the CI to get into the meeting."

"How?" she asked.

"I'm going to track the CI, and before he goes in the meeting I'll make sure he knows that he has to take me with him. By force if necessary."

"Why not just tell him who you are?" she asked.

"No need to risk it. It'll work out better if he thinks I'm on the dark side like Lucas Jones. Don't worry, I know my cover. It's one I've done numerous times before."

"What bank?"

"Tenth Street Bank downtown." Brian paused.

"And I can handle this, Max. I don't want you to get too close. We've both done ops like this before. This one will be no different."

"If the meeting goes too long, you know I'll come for you."

Brian nodded. "But you have to give me a lot of time and leeway. I'm not exactly sure what will transpire once I get inside that bank with the CI."

"Understood. But I'll still be there, regardless. How long do you want me to give you?"

"Two hours."

Max let out a breath. "Okay. But I would prefer if it was shorter."

"I don't want to work under that type of pressure, knowing you could bust in at any moment. This may be our only chance for me to try to get in with Lucas."

"And what did you tell your boss?" Max asked. "Are you still working for Tom?"

"Yeah. I told him that I was going to do an off-the-books undercover operation and that he needed to trust me. In the twelve years I've worked for him I've never made a request like that, so he understood that it had to be something big, and he didn't ask any questions. Just told me to be careful and that I couldn't expect FBI backup. Which I told him I fully understood."

"Once again, I appreciate you sticking your neck out," Max said.

"You'd do the same for me. We leave in an hour," Brian said. "But make sure you give me plenty of room to operate."

"I've got your back." Max only hoped that he wouldn't need to act.

"I'm glad you realized that I needed to come along with you," Sydney said.

"I don't trust anyone besides Brian, and I wasn't about to leave you completely by yourself. Given my reservations about Elena, I just feel better having you with me."

Sydney had been relieved she hadn't had to fight him on it. She felt so much safer being by his side. And she prayed for Brian's safety as he got ready to go to the meeting.

They sat in the car parked a block down from the bank in metered parking. She clutched her hands in her lap. It was nighttime, but the bright downtown streetlights illuminated the area.

"There," Max said. "Rounding the corner is Brian and the confidential informant. They're about to go in the bank."

"I wonder where Brian found him."

"He has his ways. I told you he's good."

"Is Lucas already inside?" she asked. Her hands were clammy in anticipation.

"No. Since it's after hours, the CI will open up the door and let Lucas in."

She could hear herself breathing in and out as the minutes ticked by in silence. "I wonder what's taking so long?"

"We have to just wait it out."

"Is there another entrance that we can't see from our vantage point?"

"Not one that can be accessed after hours. Brian checked on all of that."

"All right," she replied softly.

"No need to worry just yet." He reached over and gave her hand a squeeze.

She tried to tell herself to get a grip. She was totally safe with Max. They were in his car, and nothing was going to happen to her. She kept her eyes focused on the area surrounding the bank.

A few minutes later her world stopped. Her breath caught as she physically recoiled in her seat.

"That's Lucas Jones," Max said as he pointed at two men walking toward the bank. "It's just like we've planned, Sydney. No need to be worried. He can't even see us."

"No," she said softly. "The man beside Jones."

"What about him? A guy like Jones rarely

travels alone. He will always have some type of security with him. That's just how they operate."

She pushed down the wave of nausea that threatened to overtake her. "He's not just anyone, Max. That man is my ex-boyfriend." She paused as she continued to fight the urge to flee. "That's Rick Ward."

Max quickly straightened up in his seat. "Are you sure?"

"P-positive," she stuttered. "I'd recognize that man anywhere."

"Well, this complicates things," Max said.

"I thought you said there was no current information linking Rick to the East River gang."

Max blew out a breath. "I did tell you that. But the source of that information was Davies."

"Oh, no," she said.

He reached over and touched her shoulder. "We can't jump to any conclusions."

She started to to shake. The man who had abused her was definitely involved in this. There was no questioning it now. Just as she had no doubt he'd kill her. "I know you have to say that, but it all has to be connected. Rick gets out of prison and takes right back up with East River. He wants his chance at revenge. Against me."

"I won't let that happen. Do you hear me?"

She nodded.

"Right now I just need to keep my eyes on that building and the clock. The two hours has started."

Sydney felt like the hands on her watch stood still. She didn't know what to say. What could she say? That she was terrified that the man who had taken so much from her was back to take it all? That when the time came would she really be willing to stand her ground and take on the man who'd injured her both physically and emotionally?

She looked over at Max who remained focused and calm amidst the latest developments. After an hour had passed, she was getting restless. "Can I get out and stretch my legs just for a minute?"

"Sure," he said. "I'll get out, too, but you can't go anywhere. Stay right beside the car."

"That's fine. I just want to stand for a minute." She was having a hard time remaining calm sitting so still in the car. What she wouldn't give for a nice jog right now to expend some of her nervous energy.

People milled about on the streets, but it wasn't crowded. Taking in a few deep breaths of fresh air settled her a bit.

"Get back in the car now, Sydney!"

Max's sharp tone broke her out of her

thoughts. She did as he said without question, and turned to look. "What's going on?"

He jumped in the driver seat, started the car and pulled away. "We've got company."

"How do you know?"

"I think it's law enforcement in an unmarked car. I saw a guy get in his car as soon as you got out. It was like he recognized who you were."

She wanted nothing more than to flee the scene. But then she remembered. "What about Brian?"

"He's on his own for now. I've got to get you out of here." He paused. "Hang on because this could get dicey."

She gripped her seat, but she couldn't help herself. She had to turn around. "I don't see anyone."

"Doesn't mean they're not coming. If it is law enforcement, he could've called it in and tagged our car and plates. We may have cops on top of us as at any moment."

"No, we can't let that happen."

He punched the gas. "I hope Elena isn't behind this little stunt."

"Why would you think it was her?"

"Because she'd be the only one who would focus on Brian's whereabouts."

"We don't even know if it's anything. It could be unrelated." She craned her neck to see out the rear window. "I still don't even see anyone tailing us, Max."

Max didn't respond but instead floored it as he weaved through the city streets, then hit the interstate and headed north.

After a few minutes, she looked back again. "Doesn't look like we were followed."

Max ran a hand through his hair keeping the other on the wheel. "I'm so sorry, Sydney. Maybe I was just imagining things."

She smiled. The conscientious marshal wasn't as unshakeable as he let on. "It's completely understandable that you'd be overly cautious, and I'm grateful. So where does this leave us?"

"I'm going to circle back and head to Brian's house. Make a cautious approach there just in case. Then we'll just have to wait for him."

"Sounds like a plan." She only hoped that Brian made it back.

Max was worried he was losing it. By acting with his emotions, something he normally wouldn't do, he'd left Brian without backup. The more he replayed the events in his head, the more he was convinced that the person he saw had nothing to do with Sydney or the investigation. He was imagining threats where none existed. He just hoped it wouldn't cost

Brian his life. He would never forgive himself for the misjudgment if it did.

He was sitting in the living room waiting on any word from Brian. It'd been almost three hours since Brian went inside the bank, and Max was worried.

When they had returned to Brian's, he'd conducted a security sweep and determined all was safe. Sydney had opted to lie down for a few minutes and rest. But Max was far too keyed up for that, replaying the night's events over and over again in his mind.

He paused for a moment and wondered how Sydney was managing to keep her cool. Yeah, no doubt she'd been getting antsy waiting in the car—and understandably so after she'd seen Ward. But once Max had lost it and driven them away, she'd regained her composure quickly. Was it her faith that made her so strong?

Max knew where his strength came from—it came from within. But with Sydney it was as if she had an extra layer of courage. Her faith was definitely helping her. And by helping her stay calm it was helping him, too.

She'd told him earlier that she was praying for him. A part of him almost welcomed those prayers. But that didn't mean he could return to his faith, did it?

His mind wandered back to his youth and sitting in church where he'd been so interested in the sermons. What ultimately had turned him off from faith? Had it been the actual ideas... or had it been his parents?

The door slammed, closing off those thoughts, and he jumped, almost knocking over his glass of soda.

He breathed out a sigh of relief when he saw Brian. "What happened?" Max asked.

"I could ask you the same thing. You were nowhere to be found when I walked out of the bank."

Max stood up. "There was a false alarm. I thought we had been made, so I got Sydney out of there. I'm sorry I left you hanging, but since I wasn't sure, I didn't feel it was safe to double back to the bank."

Brian nodded. "Well, the meeting was a lot more than I bargained for. I can tell you that much."

"And you don't even know all of it."

Brian walked over to him, his eyes wide with concern. "I was hoping you could shed some light on why Jones's hired muscle came to me at the end of the meeting with a proposal."

"What kind of proposal?"

"A deadly one."

SEVEN

Sydney walked down the stairs just in time to hear the ominous words come out of Brian's mouth. Her heartbeat raced. "What do you mean?"

Both men turned and looked at her with deep frowns on their faces.

"You can go back and rest. I'll catch you up later," Max told her.

She shook her head as she entered the living room. "No way. This is all about me. I deserve to know the truth."

"Well, I tend to agree," Brian said. "But someone's going to have to help me fill in the blanks."

She felt Max's eyes on her, assessing her. She nodded and he turned to Brian. "Ask away."

"All right. Well, the guy with Lucas Jones was named Rick Ward. And after I was done talking to Jones, he approached me about using my resources to track down and kill someone." His eyes darkened as he turned to her. "You, Sydney."

She wasn't the least bit surprised. It was just as she suspected. Rick wouldn't rest until she had been punished for what she'd done to him. She'd embarrassed him by running out on him when he'd never expected she'd have the nerve or the courage to leave him. "Brian, that man you met is my ex-boyfriend."

"Ward is your ex?" Brian asked with a raised eyebrow.

"Unfortunately so." She didn't really want to rehash the history with Brian, but considering all he was doing for her, he deserved to know the truth. She gave him the condensed version. "He seemed nice enough at the beginning, but then he became highly abusive. So much so that I feared for my life. One day I was able to make a break for it, so I did."

"I'm so sorry, Sydney. But now this makes a lot more sense to me. It seemed very personal for Ward. And we had this conversation after Lucas Jones had left the room. Ward was very intent on getting this job done whatever the cost. He offered me one hundred thousand."

"How did you respond to Ward?" Max asked.

"I told him I'd think about it, but that I'd want a better deal than that, as well as access to Jones."

Then it hit her. "I have an idea."

Max walked over to where she stood. "What is it?"

"Have Brian agree to this deal with Ward."

"What?" the men asked in unison.

"We'll fake my death." She stood with her hands on her hips, proud of her idea.

"No way," Max said. "It's way too risky. Ward is the type of guy that will want proof."

"We'll have to come up with something," she told him. "But just think about it. It's the perfect plan. It gets Ward off my back and gives Brian time to investigate the link between Diaz and Jones."

"And how do you suppose that we'll make the US Marshals think you're dead?" Max asked. "They're still looking for us."

"All the more reason to go on the run. Get away from here." She looked at Brian, hoping he'd back up her idea.

"She may have a point," Brian said. "It could be a great plan."

Max threw his hands in the air. "Maybe in the abstract. But I'm telling you, the details of faking her death make me very nervous. How are you going to convince Ward that you killed Sydney?"

Brian remained calm as he defended his opinion. "We've done things like this before."

"But this is different," Max said.

"But it's doable," Brian countered.

As the men argued, Sydney grew more certain of her plan. Feeling as though she could fight back against Rick was empowering. Maybe it wouldn't be with her fists, but this would be even better.

Finally, Brian seemed to win out. He calmly explained how he'd make Sydney's plan work. "Ward is supposed to get back to me with a new quote for my dirty work and a guarantee of another meeting with Jones. I didn't want to seem desperate to work with them. I think Lucas Jones and I had a good talk. But it's going to take more than one meeting to get what I need from him. Guys like him don't divulge critical details in the first meeting. Sydney's plan would buy me the additional time to work on the connections."

She clasped her hands together in front of her. "So it sounds like it's settled to me. We're going to do this. Now it's just a matter of logistics."

Max scoffed. "If only the logistics weren't the hardest part."

"What about Elena?" Sydney asked.

"I think we have to keep her in the dark. The only people that can know the truth right now are the three of us."

"Well, we better sit down and get to work," Brian said.

They gathered around the table, developing a plan of action. Sydney loved the fact that they were going on the offensive as opposed to waiting for something else awful to happen.

Brian ordered three large pizzas, mainly because he and Max claimed they were starving. Now with two pizzas decimated and a third being worked on, it seemed like the right choice. She'd even polished off three slices of pepperoni.

"Now, about proving my death," she said, wiping her hands on a napkin. "Maybe Brian could take a piece of my clothing and a lock of my hair."

"I don't know if that would be enough."

"Could we stage a picture?" she asked.

"We could definitely do that," Brian said. "That could be my backup if he doesn't go for the tangible articles."

"What about timing?" she asked.

Brian looked at her. "Ward wanted it done ASAP. Like I said, it was clear he had it in for you. Once he gets back to me with his revised offer, which could be as soon as tonight, then I'll tell him I'll get started."

"Either way, this will be our last night here. We're going to move," Max said.

"That's smart. Are you sure you'll be okay for the rest of night? Are you still good with Elena?"

"*Good* may be too strong of a word, but I think if she wanted to do something, she would've already done it. I just have to make sure we're not followed when we leave."

Brian seemed unsettled. "Maybe you should leave now. Are you awake enough to drive for an hour or so?"

"Of course," Max said. "And come to think about it, I agree with you." He turned to Sydney. "Pack up your things."

"I picked up two burner phones." Brian handed one to Max. "I programmed my burner number into yours."

"Great," Max said.

"Before you leave, though, I need to get the picture of Sydney and her things."

These guys were professionals. Sydney was in the best possible hands given the gravity of the situation. And even though she couldn't stop being anxious, she felt a lot better knowing that they had a plan. Especially a plan that involved making Ward think she was dead. It wouldn't solve her problem forever, but at least it would be a temporary solution.

Sydney awoke the next morning with a start. Where was she? Then it came back to her.

They'd driven into South Carolina and stopped in the middle of the night so that Max could get some much needed rest.

The night had passed by in a blur as she had cut off a lock of her hair and then posed for the picture to fake her death. Brian had been careful about the picture, setting up the angle and the lighting that would make it the most realistic. As a professional forensic artist, she felt a bit strange being the subject of the photo and not being able to provide her expert input. What was even more troubling was the fact that if she had stayed with Rick, she might be dead right now instead of just posing as if she was.

Max and Brian insisted that they got a shot that could fool Rick. Rick wasn't stupid, but his arrogance often clouded his intelligence. He used his size and strength to get his way and not his brain.

As she lay in the hotel-room bed, she couldn't help but think about how she'd ever ended up with a man like Rick Ward in the first place. But there was no use thinking about it now. That was the past. And because of what had happened with Rick, she'd found faith. Her life had forever changed.

But her heart still ached because of something else. Someone else. What if the Lord had put Max in her life for a reason? What if she could be to him what others had been to her? Max had lived a Christian life for years and had only turned away because of his difficult childhood. Did the Lord want her to help bring Max back to faith?

She could only continue to pray that God would give her the strength and wisdom to know how to handle the situation. To show Max that returning to his faith would actually be freeing and empowering. That how his parents lived wasn't the way he had to live.

One thing was for certain. She wasn't giving up on Max. He was her friend and always would be—if they made it through this alive. And she wanted to have the opportunity for him to continue to see how God worked through her life. No doubt it would be an uphill battle, but one she was ready for.

But was she ready for Rick and the East River gang to continue their pursuit? She wasn't sure, but she knew she'd get through it. And when this was over, she wanted Rick to face justice for what he'd done to her. Because if he had treated her that way, he surely had done the same thing to other women.

A knock on the adjoining door had her jumping up out of the bed and throwing on a sweater over her T-shirt. She looked at the clock and saw it was almost 10:00 a.m.

"Hey." She opened the door, and Max stood there with a faint smile.

"I slept like a rock," he said. "But I guess I needed it."

"Yeah, we didn't get in last night until after one."

"How are you feeling?" He stepped inside her room.

"Considering everything that's happened, I'm holding up pretty good."

He grabbed her hand. "You are strong."

"Thanks." She felt her heart warm, whether at his words of praise or at his touch, she didn't know.

"You must be starving. I know I am. Want to grab some food?"

"Yeah, can you just give me a few minutes to hop in the shower?"

"Of course. Knock on my door when you're ready."

When he let her hand go and walked out of her room, she realized her heart was pounding. And it had nothing to do with danger—and all to do with Max.

Max exhaled after he left Sydney's room. With each passing day his respect for her grew. The strength and courage she had demonstrated throughout this ordeal was amazing. But he wondered if he was starting to feel something else for her.

How was that even possible, though? He'd had casual relationships before, but there had never been any authentic emotion. He felt as if he understood Sydney more than any of those other women. And even more strangely, he felt like Sydney got him.

His burner phone buzzed, and he picked it up.

"Hey," he said, knowing it had to be Brian.

"I've got good news. The operation is a go. Ward took the bait. I told him I'd have the job completed ASAP and would send him proof as soon as it was done. I'm also supposed to meet with Jones again tonight."

"How are you feeling about things?"

"Actually pretty solid. I think this plan just may work. I'll have to feel out Jones to determine how much to push the Kevin Diaz angle. I set it up to where I'd be worried about Diaz being my competition. But I don't want to come off as too nosy or it may send up red flags. I'll have to go with my gut once I hear what Jones has to say."

"I get that, but we also don't have a lot of time here. We can't risk that trial restarting without Sydney's testimony against Kevin Diaz. Once word gets out to Diaz that Sydney is dead, he'll think he's home free on the charges. Without her expert testimony, the state's case isn't that strong."

"I understand, man. I'll do all I can and then some."

Max took a deep breath. "I know. I appreciate this more than you can ever know."

Brian didn't reply right away. A few seconds passed, and when he did speak, his voice was different, more tentative. "Max, is something deeper going on between you and Sydney?"

"What do you mean?"

"I've known you for years. And there's something about the way you are around her that's different."

Max didn't want to go down this road because he didn't fully understand it himself just yet. But he wasn't about to tell Brian that, either. He responded as any marshal would. "I just want to do everything in my power to protect her."

"Understood, bro. Be careful. I'll update you as soon as I can."

Knowing the plan was set into motion, Max ended the call and paced for the few minutes until Sydney was ready. They opted for the fast-food drive-through and brought back an assortment of things to the hotel. They ate in her room since she had the bigger table.

"I'm glad they let us order breakfast and lunch. I'm starving." Sydney laughed as she eyed the array of food.

It was great seeing her smile and laugh. Over the past few days there had been few opportunities to do so. Her smile reached all the way to her big brown eyes and seemed to light up her face, making her even prettier.

They ate in silence. When they were done he wasn't sure why he broached the topic he did.

"I know you said that you found a church after you left Ward. But before all that happened with him, what was your stance on faith?"

Her eyes widened. He'd definitely surprised her with that question. "You know, I didn't really have a stance. I guess I'd say I was neutral. My mom never took me to church. Sadly, she died a few years ago." She paused. "So, growing up I didn't have any example to go by. But I wouldn't say that I was as skeptical as you are. I never had the experience of believing and then wanting to walk away from faith."

"I am skeptical," he concurred. "But I have reason to be."

"What happened to you, Max?"

He looked down. "I don't really like talking about it."

"You have walls around you. Believe me, I

get that. But I think you realize at this point that I wouldn't judge your past."

He knew she wouldn't. Feeling safe with her, he decided to divulge a bit of his life. "I told you that I grew up going to church. My family was all about show. In the community, they were highly respected. But at home it was a very different story. Both of my parents had issues that led them to being unavailable. My mom was hooked on pain pills and my dad to his job and, unfortunately, other women. I never experienced any physical abuse like you did, but my childhood was filled with apathy. Smiles outside the house and very few words spoken inside the house."

"That's a tough way to grow up," she said.

"When I got older it was hard for me to understand how they could claim to be believers when they couldn't even show the smallest bit of love toward me—their only child. A complete lack of concern. That is, unless it had something to do with how the community saw me. I had to do exactly what they wanted to be the perfect child."

"I'm so sorry, Max. Every child deserves to be loved."

"Sydney, I have to say that seeing how you have carried yourself during this entire crisis has made me more curious about how faith works for you. I can't help but wonder, what if I was wrong? What if I've been too hasty to throw out all religion because of the experiences I lived through?"

"It's not too late, Max. If you feel like the Lord is calling out to you, then He probably is."

"You've shown me through your actions and words what it's really like to live by faith. And now a return to my faith is something that I'm interested in exploring further. Believe it or not, as a child I enjoyed church. It wasn't until I got older that the experience became tainted for me."

"I'm here, Max. For whatever you need. You're risking your life for me. The least I can do is lend an ear."

"Syd, I appreciate everything."

Silence overtook them as she cleaned up her food wrappers. As she went to gather his trash, he reached up and gently touched her face. "My promise to you has always been the same. To keep you safe."

"I know, Max. Thank you."

As he looked into her eyes, he was amazed at how his life continued to change all because she had come into it. And he wasn't going to let her down.

Sydney sat quietly in the passenger's seat as the car sped down the highway to an unknown destination. She couldn't stop thinking about their earlier conversation. Her heart had almost exploded at Max's words about his past and how she had influenced him spiritually. For a man like Max, who not only had misgivings about religion but prided himself on his logical approach, this was a big breakthrough. She would continue to pray for him and live her life the only way she knew how.

But even with Max's desire to return to his faith, she wouldn't allow herself to think there could ever be anything more than friendship between the two of them. While she trusted Max in his role as her friend and protector, trusting in a romantic sense was a different matter entirely. She truly believed that her heart might not ever be ready for romance again.

It hurt a bit that he was skeptical about her work as a sketch artist. She was proud of all of her accomplishments as a forensic artist— including the sketch-artist work. Just because he'd had one bad experience didn't mean that she couldn't do her job and do it well.

Max's phone rang from the console.

"Put it on speaker, will you?" he asked. "That has to be Brian."

She picked up the phone and pressed the speaker button.

"Brian," Max said. "What's going on?"

"It's not Brian," a deep male voice responded.

"Who is this?" Max asked. He kept the car on the road, but Sydney could see the anger streaking through him as he clenched his hands on the steering wheel.

"I'm disappointed that you forgot about me so quickly, buddy."

"Davies. What are you doing?"

"I could ask you the same thing, but for now here's what's going to happen. I have your FBI pal here with me."

Max blew out a breath. Sydney knew this was bad. Their entire operation had been compromised. How had this happened? Her heart thumped wildly as she worried about Brian's safety.

"What do you want?" Max asked.

"A trade. Sydney for your FBI agent."

Before she could react, Max replied, "When and where?"

"Your response was so quick, I almost believe you." Davies laughed. "I know you're going to want to save the day—to keep your witness safe and rescue Brian—but you're smart enough to know that won't happen. Especially if you pull any fast ones. So you're going to do this exactly as I say if you don't want me to put a bullet through your friend's brain."

She noticed Max's jaw clench as Davies

spoke. Then he ground out, "Tell me how this will go down."

"I don't know where you are, but you need to get yourself back to Atlanta. I'll text you an address and time later today."

The call ended and Sydney realized she had been holding her breath. She hit the End button. "What happened?"

"I don't know. But Brian's in trouble. They have his phone and they know who he is."

She was almost afraid to ask the next question. "They're going to kill him, anyway, aren't they?"

"Unfortunately, there's a good chance that might happen, but I'm obviously not going to hand you over to them under any circumstances."

"But what about Brian?"

"We'll figure out something, but we need to go back to Atlanta. And I need to call Elena. I'm not going to be able to do this alone."

"You're not alone, Max."

He looked over at her briefly and nodded. "I know that, Sydney. But my priority hasn't changed. Your safety is still not only my job, but it's what I need to do." He asked her to dial Elena's number, which Max had committed to memory.

She dialed and put it on speaker.

"Sanchez," Elena answered.

"Hey, it's Max."

"Where in the world are you? I thought we agreed you'd let me know before you left Brian's house."

"I never agreed to that." He paused. "But we have bigger problems than that right now. Brian went on an undercover operation to get evidence tying Lucas Jones to Kevin Diaz. And somewhere in all of that Davies got involved and was able to figure out Brian was FBI. They have him."

"Oh, no," she said. "Why didn't you bring me in on this at the beginning of the op?"

"I'm sorry if I was still a bit hesitant about trusting you given all that had gone on."

"I know, Max. And I'll be apologizing to you and Sydney forever about that. But I promise you that I'm on your side."

"Well, at this point I don't have much of a choice but to trust you. Davies says that unless I turn over Sydney, he'll kill Brian. Davies is going to send me a meeting time and place later today."

"You can't give over your witness," Elena said in a commanding tone.

"Obviously not. That's where you come in. You're going to be the decoy."

Sydney was just as shocked as Elena.

"What?" Elena's eyes widened. "It isn't like Sydney and I look a lot alike."

"We'll make it work."

Without hesitating, Elena replied, "You're right. I'm partially responsible for this mess. I'll do whatever it takes. Is Sydney doing okay?"

"I'm right here," Sydney said, trying to keep her voice from shaking. "I'm fine."

"Max, Davies has to have something else planned, though," Elena said. "He can't really think that you'd actually give him Sydney, even if it was to save Brian's life."

"You're right," he replied. "But we have to play by his rules for now."

"I'm on board."

"Elena, we also found out that Ward is definitely working with East River," Max said.

"What? I thought the FBI didn't have any information connecting them since Ward's release from prison."

"Well, that information was given to us by Davies."

Elena groaned. "Yes, I remember now. The problem is that I'm still no better off here than I was. I can't say for certain that there aren't other dirty marshals."

"We might be able to go to Brian's boss, and my old boss, Tom Hilton at the FBI. Brian didn't tell him anything about the op, but the guy's pretty open-minded when it comes to operations. Maybe he'll help us."

"Are you sure that he's clean?" Elena asked.

"No, but we might not have a choice."

"I'll reach out to Hilton," Elena said. "Assuming you're all right with that, Max?"

"Sure. Elena, now's not the time for us to have a lack of trust. Once I made this phone call to you, I had made the decision that I was going to trust you. So we need to be able to move forward together as a team to get this job done. Dwelling on the past isn't going to help any of us right now."

"Thanks, Max. I'll let you know what I find out. I'll also find us a place to meet."

"Talk to you soon."

Sydney ended the call and glanced over at Max.

He flicked his gaze to her. "Well, looks like we're headed back to Georgia."

"I should've known it was too good to be true. There's no getting away from that monster. From my past. From all the danger that surrounds us both."

He grabbed her left hand with his right, keeping his other hand on the wheel. "Sydney, I promise you that I will do everything I can to ensure that Ward never hurts you again."

"That's a big statement," she said softly.

He shook his head. "I'm not going to change the way I feel about that. I'll protect you whatever it takes."

"I know that, but Rick truly is an evil man. I pray each day to forgive him and to move on with my life, but if I'm being completely honest with you, I haven't gotten past it. I don't know if I ever will. I don't know if I'll ever be strong enough to forgive him."

"Well, I'm obviously not the expert on prayer, but I'll tell you this. He hasn't asked for your forgiveness. He hired what he thought was a hit man to kill you. So I don't think you should feel obligated."

"It's not good for me to feel the hatred I do for him. I know that logically, but emotionally it's more difficult to process."

"I think you're doing the best you can under incredibly difficult circumstances. Most people would've crumbled by now, especially with him back in the picture. But you haven't. And you won't. Because that's who you are."

She offered a tentative smile. "You act like you know me pretty well."

"While it hasn't been very long, I do feel like I know you. Even better than people who've been in my life for years. Being with you has made getting to know you easy. If that makes sense."

"I feel the same way. As tough as all of these issues are, we seem to be working through them."

"Day by day," he said. "Along with the rest of this madness."

Somehow Max's words settled her, as they always did. His presence had a calming effect on her. "Can I ask you a question?"

"Sure," he said.

"Why did you leave the FBI to go to the US Marshals?"

He let out a laugh. "I don't know what I thought you were going to ask me, but it definitely wasn't that."

"I'm sorry if you don't want to talk about it. I was just wondering."

"No, it's nothing like that. I'd been at the FBI for ten years. I enjoyed my job, but I felt a bit boxed in. I didn't really feel challenged the way I used to. I'd done a lot of undercover work and really enjoyed it, but there were a lot of management demands that came with more seniority. I was behind the desk more and more. Pushing paper and other desk work in the bureaucracy is not my strength."

She couldn't help but laugh loudly. "Right, I can't even imagine you sitting behind a desk all day. You excel working out on assignments in the field."

"So when this opportunity opened up at the US Marshals, I thought, why not apply? See what happens. My boss was on board with it and thought it would be a good change of pace for me. I wanted something new that would allow me to be on my feet more. I realize I won't want to be this active forever. I want to embrace it now while I'm still relatively young."

"How old are you?"

"Thirty-three." He shot her a smile. "And I know better than to ask a woman her age."

"I'm not most women. I'm thirty and I'm not ashamed of that."

"Believe me, Syd. I realized how different you were from day one."

EIGHT

Max felt his blood pressure rising with each passing moment. He was seated at a table in an FBI safe house in Atlanta. Around the table sat Elena, Sydney and Brian's boss, Special Agent in Charge Tom Hilton.

Sydney had barely said a word since they'd walked in, but Tom had a lot of questions and concerns. And Elena was trying to take the temperature down in the room, but it didn't appear to be working.

"When Brian told me about his undercover operation, I had no idea he'd be putting himself in this much risk," Tom said. "Had I known, I would've specifically forbidden it."

Max was about to speak up, but Tom kept right on going.

"And there's an APB out for the two of you." Tom pointed to him and Sydney. "Max, I don't have any idea what you've gone and done here. So someone needs to start at the beginning and tell me everything." Tom's light blue eyes were full of intensity. Max knew the seasoned FBI agent wasn't going to be easy to deal with. But they needed him as an ally.

It took about an hour between Max and Elena's explanations and Tom's questions to get him caught up to speed. Tom confirmed a few points specifically with Sydney as they went.

"And where is Davies now?" he asked Max.

"I don't know, sir. He's supposed to text me a time and place to make the exchange." He looked at his watch. "It's almost eight p.m. now, but Davies correctly assumed we weren't in Atlanta and that it would take us a number of hours to get back."

"What's your theory on how Brian's cover was blown?" Tom asked.

Max shrugged. "Davies isn't stupid. He was probably skeptical of Brian from the start. I think Davies probably decided to try to make sure Brian was legitimate and in that process was able to figure out he was working undercover." He ran a hand through his hair. "But how did Davies get out of the hospital so quickly?" He looked at Elena.

"I'm not sure," she said.

"I'm more concerned about what we're going to do now," Tom said. "I can bring in additional FBI resources."

"We have to be careful, sir," Max said. "We don't know if any of the agents have been compromised by East River."

"I'd handpick the team myself," he said. "So there wouldn't be any concern about that."

"Think about it. If we're wrong about any of those guys, then Brian is dead. We've got to give him a fighting chance."

Tom looked down for a moment and the room was silent. Then he made eye contact with Max again. "I hear you. So for now it's you and me against them, while Elena protects the witness."

Max shook his head. "No. Elena will help you. I'm not leaving Sydney. That's nonnegotiable."

Elena must have sensed the tension building in the room. "Sydney, let's give them a couple of minutes to hash out these details."

Sydney didn't argue and left the room with Elena.

"Is there something you're not telling me, Max?"

"I think you're insinuating something, so why don't you come out with it?"

Tom crossed his hefty arms. "I'm a bit disappointed in you, Max. After all the years I've known you, I would've never expected it."

"Expected what, sir?"

Tom leaned forward. "There's something going on between you and your witness."

Max chose his words carefully. "There is, sir, but not what you think. Yes, I care about her. But we are not in a physical relationship." How else could he say it?

Tom raised a curious eyebrow. "I know we had our share of disagreements during the time that you worked for me. But I trust your instincts, and I know that Brian does, too. He wouldn't have gone on this assignment otherwise."

"Thank you, sir."

"But let's just hope you didn't send him to his death."

"Please don't say that."

"I hope not. But someone had to say it." Tom shook his head. "Back to the issue. What were you thinking the plan would be?"

"You'd go to the meet with Davies, keeping Elena far enough back to make him believe that she's Sydney."

"The problem with that is that he's going to know I'm not you."

"Will he really care as long as he thinks he's getting Sydney?"

"It will definitely raise his suspicions."

"Like I said. That point is nonnegotiable. I'm not going to leave Sydney."

Max's cell buzzed, and he picked it up to read the incoming message. "It's Davies. He just sent the address. He wants to meet at midnight tonight."

"Where?"

"The address is 55 Century Park. It's in Atlanta. But that street doesn't mean anything to me."

Tom pulled out his smartphone and typed in the address. He gave his phone to Max and pointed. "There it is. On the south side past the airport. Basically, it's an industrial zone with some local manufacturing plants. Lots of trucks and warehouses down that way."

"So I'm thinking that you'll get out to meet Davies, leaving Elena in the car. You tell him that you have to see Brian first before you'll do anything."

"Davies knows how the FBI and marshals work. He'll know that we would never turn over an innocent civilian in exchange for an FBI agent."

Max stood and started pacing. "True, which means our main goal at this point in the operation should be to apprehend Davies. And we have to be prepared for anything. That this could be a trap of some sort. Davies knows protocol, and he has to know that if he dangled Brian in front of us, we'd have to agree to a meeting. For all we know Brian may already be dead. At the very least, there's no guarantee that Davies will actually bring Brian with him to the meeting. You're just going to have to go with your gut. I'll be there, but I won't be able to get too close."

"We better explain the plan to Elena and Sydney." Tom rose from his chair. "We'll also want to get there well in advance of midnight. Especially so I can scout out the best place for me to be."

"You're right."

"Go get Elena and Sydney so we can brief them," Tom ordered. "It's going to be a long night."

Sydney knew she had to be prepared for anything. She and Max sat in the car in what seemed to be the middle of nowhere. She could smell the pungent smoke that filled the air from the manufacturing plants that surrounded the entire area.

Max and Tom had briefed her and Elena on the plan. A plan she didn't like because she wanted a more active role. She hated sitting on the sidelines, feeling as though she was the cause of everyone's problems. Not only had she been trained in self-defense, but she also knew how to shoot. And she was a good shot.

She'd convinced Tom to get her a gun for tonight, and she had the feeling that this operation might go south.

She watched Max use his FBI night-vision goggles Tom had provided. Tom seemed to be completely prepared for anything, as he had a basement full of supplies. She guessed someone in his position had to take every precaution.

She scanned the area. It wasn't very well lit and just thinking about the implications of everything had her on edge. A chill shot down her arms in anticipation of what was to come.

"How're you doing?" Max asked.

"I'm fine. Don't worry about me. I'm ready to take action if I need to. I won't just sit back and watch others get hurt because of me."

Max shook his head. "Remember what we all talked about. Just because you have that gun doesn't mean you're supposed to use it. That's only for protection and not for anything else."

"I know that, but I feel better knowing that I have it." She looked down at her watch, struggling to see the time.

"It's almost midnight," he said.

"Thanks." They were in his car stationed behind one of the 18-wheelers. But they had a line of sight to where Tom and Elena's SUV was parked, which was directly in front of the address Davies had provided.

The minutes passed slowly as she waited and watched. Then another SUV drove up and parked near Tom's.

"Game time," Max said. "Stay alert and listen to any cues I may give."

"Got it." Sydney had her gun out just in case. She wasn't taking any chances. She tried to breathe normally, but it was difficult. *Lord, please keep us safe here tonight.* She controlled her breathing and stayed focused.

"That's Davies," Max said.

Sydney watched as a man stepped out of the driver side of the SUV. She didn't have night-vision goggles, but he fit Davies's body description.

Tom hopped out of his SUV and the two men walked toward each other. Sydney wanted desperately to hear what they were saying, but all she could do was try to read their body language.

After a minute Tom took a step back. And that's when everything changed. Gunshots rang out—from where, she couldn't tell. Multiple shots were being fired at the SUV—with Elena inside it.

"Do something, Max!" she implored.

"I'm not leaving you here alone."

"I'm fine. I've got my gun. You've got to help them. Now."

More gunshots rang out in rapid succession. Tom ran for cover behind a nearby building, and Davies retreated toward his SUV. Three men ran toward the SUV that held Elena.

"Go, Max. Go!"

Max jumped out of the car and drew his gun. He started shooting, taking down the first man with a shot to the leg, and the second man with a shot to the shoulder. Even at that distance Max was a stellar shot.

She prayed that Elena hadn't been hit by the attackers' bullets.

A loud tapping sounded on her window, she turned and her heart stopped.

Staring at her with a gun pointed right at her face was her biggest nightmare—Rick Ward.

"Get out of the car now, Sydney," he said.

He must not have seen her gun as it was cloaked in the darkness. She actually had the upper hand. But what if she made a move and he was quicker? What if he shot first? She weighed her options as he stared at her through the window.

"Don't make any sudden moves. Get out nice and easy," he said. His eyes were filled with pure hatred, and it took every bit of her strength not to curl up in a ball and give up. But no. She wasn't that woman anymore. She was going to fight back. She hadn't trained and fought to become strong to let him see her weakness now when it mattered most.

Given the situation, she decided it was now or never. She had to catch him off guard while she could.

"Okay," she said, keeping her voice calm and steady. She moved slowly to unlock the door. Then with all of her strength, she swung open the door making him stumble backward. She drew her gun and didn't hesitate. She got off a quick shot, but he was able to duck just in time and she missed by a few inches.

She fired again, and he was thrown off balance dodging her bullet. He hit the ground, his gun falling out of his hand. She was about to take another shot when he stood up and charged her like a raging bull. This time she did hesitate for a second—one second too long. He knocked her to the ground hard with him on top of her. The gun fell out of her grasp.

Here she was again. In a place she'd prepared and trained for years to handle but prayed she would never have to be. Fighting with this man. But one thing had changed. She was no longer afraid and unable to protect herself. No longer defenseless against him or any other man wanting to do her harm.

Her training and instincts all kicked into action. Even though he was on top of her pressing his weight down, she knew what to do. He had her arms pinned to the ground, but her legs were her best and strongest defense. She'd learned that the first day of her most basic self-defense class. So when he lifted up slightly she took the opportunity to act.

In one well-practiced motion, her left knee slammed into his stomach as she pushed as hard as she could against his hip with her right leg. He hadn't seen that coming, she thought, as she was able to get to her feet. Her instructor would have been proud.

But now she'd made Rick angry.

"Where did you learn your little moves, Sydney?" he spat out. "You think taking one little self-defense class taught by some idiot at a rec center is going to keep you safe from me?" He laughed, but it was a laugh filled with hatred and evil.

Little did he know she hadn't just taken basic self-defense. Yeah, that's where she'd started, but it wasn't where she ended. Over the years she'd moved on to advanced martial-arts training. And she was prepared to use those moves on him now.

She looked over, but the gun was still out of her reach.

He lunged toward her but she quickly side-stepped, avoiding his grip. Then she delivered a strong kick to his shin. He dropped to his knee and spouted words so foul that she never wanted to hear them again.

But now wasn't the time to cower. While he was kneeling down, she delivered another swift kick, this one to his head. He rolled over and howled. But he grabbed her ankle, yanking her down to the ground hard. Dirt filled her mouth mixed with the taste of blood.

She rolled over and got back to her feet as he staggered up off the ground.

"I have to admit, this is almost fun," Rick said as he breathed hard. "I'm enjoying this new side of you, Sydney. You've become fiery."

Hearing those words sent a jolt of energy through her body. She wasn't going to let this man make a mockery of her. Out of the corner of her eye she saw her gun not far from where she stood. She made a move for it as he lunged toward her with his hands open wide, reaching.

She was able to grab the gun, but he pushed her down, and they wrestled on the ground. Using her training, she managed to get the upper hand. A part of her wanted to kill him, yet something held her back. She'd come so far and taking his life wouldn't do anything to heal her wounds. So when she had the kill shot she didn't take it.

Instead she jumped up off him and pointed the gun at his head.

When he dove toward her she took the shot, but purposely recalibrated and aimed for his leg. He hit the ground yelping in pain. But likely she'd only grazed him.

Strong hands grabbed her from behind. She struggled against them.

"It's me, Syd. We've got to get out of here," Max said.

"What about him?" she yelled.

"Leave him. East River is sending in reinforcements. We've got to get out of here right now."

"This isn't over," Rick yelled, adding a few nasty words as he writhed on the ground.

She jumped in the car and Max sped off. She looked down and realized her hands were shaking as she held on tightly to the gun.

"Sydney, talk to me," Max said.

"I fought him," she said. Hot tears rolled down her face at the enormity of what had just happened. "I stood up to him."

"I'm so proud of you. And I'm so sorry I left you alone."

"It wasn't your fault. He came to the car window with a gun and ordered me to get out. But he didn't see that I was armed, too."

"Did he hurt you?"

"A little but nothing like before. I hurt him worse than he hurt me." She blew out a breath. "Max, I had the shot. I could've killed him. But I didn't take it."

"You did the right thing, Sydney. Taking a life is no small thing."

"I know that. But in that millisecond when I had to choose, so many thoughts ran through my head."

"What stopped you from doing it?"

"I didn't know if I could live with myself. I've come so very far, and I didn't want to have him win. I'm better than that."

He reached over and grabbed her hand. "Yes, you are, Sydney."

She silently thanked God for getting her through that. Then it hit her that she hadn't even asked about everyone else. "What happened with you? The others? Are they okay?"

"We don't have Brian. I don't even think he was with Davies. But Davies brought more East River backup than any of us expected. He isn't even trying to hide the fact that he's full on with them now."

"What about Elena and Tom?"

"Elena was grazed by a bullet in the SUV, but she'll be fine. Tom is also okay. We're going to meet back up at the FBI safe house. Davies took another bullet, this time from Tom, but it didn't look life threatening. Seemed like Tom got him good, though, in his other shoulder. He's going to be in quite a bit of pain."

"So what was this all about, then?"

"It was about you, Sydney. This wasn't about Brian at all. Honestly, I don't even know what's happened to him. They might be keeping him just because they see him as a bargaining tool since he's an FBI agent in the gang unit. But we really don't know if he's still alive. I hate to think about what they could be doing to him."

"Me, too," she said softly. "This is all my fault."

"No. It's not your fault. It's the fault of Rick Ward and Phil Davies and everyone involved at East River. They have a two-part agenda, as I see it. Stopping you from testifying is the most important. But it appears to me that they've let Ward step in and take over where you're concerned."

"And we know what Rick's agenda is. Revenge. Making me pay. Then killing me."

"That's not going to happen, Sydney. I am beating myself up about leaving you in that car."

"It was the right call. You know it and I know it. Tom and Elena could both be dead if you hadn't gone. I held my own."

"You did a lot more than hold your own, Syd."

She thought back to Rick's reaction when she'd drawn her weapon and when she'd fought him off. "He was surprised. Shocked, really."

"About what?"

"That I was able to fight him. That I didn't just roll over and cry like I used to. The look on his face was something I'll never forget. He said such awful things to me, Max. Things that I don't know if I'll ever get out of my head."

"You can't change a man like that, Sydney. There's nothing you're ever going to be able to do about how he chooses to act."

She nodded, knowing he was right.

Back at the safe house, sitting at the big table that they'd only been at hours before, Max felt a flurry of emotions run through him. He was exhausted but nowhere near being able to think about going to sleep. The adrenaline was still pumping through his veins.

The biggest thought that played over and over again in his mind was that he'd left his witness behind. By providing backup to Tom and Elena, Sydney had been forced to fend for herself. That was not only against everything the US Marshals stood for, but it ate at him from the inside out on a deeper level. What if something had happened to her? It would've been his fault.

He was grateful for one thing—Sydney's training. It had paid off big time. She'd more than held her own with Rick. And for the first time Max wondered if God had had anything to do with it, because he was seriously starting to think God was watching over them all.

"Max, did you hear me?" Tom asked.

"Sorry, what did you say?" He watched as Elena and Sydney entered the room and took a seat at the table. Elena's arm was bandaged where the bullet had grazed it.

"I said, are you ready to talk about where we go from here?"

They'd already debriefed on what had happened earlier that evening. Now the goal was to come up with a new plan.

"We're still no closer to finding Brian or putting a stop to Davies. Or for that matter getting the evidence we need to tie Lucas Jones to Kevin Diaz."

"What if we're thinking about this the wrong way?" Sydney asked.

"What do you mean?" Tom replied.

"What if Kevin Diaz has nothing to do with the threats against me? What if it's all coming from Rick and by extension East River with the help of Davies?"

"I still believe that Diaz and Jones are connected," Max said. He wasn't willing to back down on that idea.

"That could be true," Elena added. "But that doesn't mean that Diaz was behind it all. Maybe East River saw this as an opportunity. Pure and simple. Get rid of Sydney, which helps Diaz *and* settles an old score for Ward. Who now seems to be Lucas Jones's right hand man."

Max thought about it for a minute. "I'll give it to you," he said. "That's a viable theory. The only reason we had discounted Ward's involvement with East River was because of what Davies had told us to throw us off the trail. We now know that Ward is a key member of East River."

"It makes you wonder why East River would be willing to go to such lengths to help Ward get revenge," Elena said. "Maybe Jones owed Ward a favor. We should look more into why Ward went to jail. There might be some answers to explain it. Because I can't see Lucas Jones going this far for any random member of East River." Elena thought for a moment and then voiced another question. "How did Ward elevate his status to work so closely with Jones? That's a very important piece of information we need to understand."

"What if Ward took the fall for Jones or

someone else very important in East River? That could explain it."

"This is all well and good," Tom said. "I get that you want to figure out the root cause and motivations. But in the meantime we need an immediate action plan."

"I think we have to widen the net at the FBI," Max said. "Get this manhunt off me and Sydney. Now with the four of us able to provide information about Davies's involvement, that should help. We can't operate successfully looking over our shoulders at legitimate law enforcement. We have enough threats from East River."

Tom nodded. "But I think you're going to have to go to the upper echelon of the marshals now, too. Elena, I know you were worried about this being bigger than just Davies, but we have zero evidence to support that theory. It will make everyone's life easier if we have the power and resources of the FBI and marshals behind us instead of against us. I'm willing to go with you to talk to whoever we need to talk to at the marshals to get this all straightened out."

"Sounds like a plan," she said.

"Why don't we all grab a few hours of sleep?

Then we'll go deal with the FBI and marshals," Tom said.

Everyone agreed. Tom and Elena left the room talking about logistics on dealing with their respective agencies, leaving Max alone with Sydney.

"You still doing all right?" he asked.

"Yes, but now I think fatigue is starting to set in."

He walked over to her and took her hand as she stood up. Then he placed his hands on her shoulders. "I can't tell you how glad I am that you're standing here right now, safe. Thinking otherwise makes me sick."

"Then don't think it. I'm here and I'm okay."

He took a step back. "You should get some rest."

"You, too."

She started to walk away, and he grabbed her hand again. He had a question he wanted to ask. "Syd, do you think God was watching over you out there?"

She smiled and gripped his hand tightly. "I know He was."

Would God be willing to watch over him, too? And someone else? "I hope he's watching over Brian, too. I can't even process if…" He started to get choked up.

"Try to stay positive and not focus on the what-ifs. I'll say an extra prayer for Brian tonight."

"Syd, it's really been on my mind since we last talked about it. What would I need to do if I wanted to go back to my faith—to being a Christian like I was as a child? Is that something I can just do?"

"It's never too late, Max. God is forgiving and will take you back if that's really what you want."

"I know I'm not perfect, but I really want to start over. I want to put my trust in the Lord again. I've thought a lot about it, and I'm ready to embrace my faith."

Her heart filled with joy. "That's wonderful, Max. As I told you, it wasn't until all of that craziness happened with Rick that I found faith. So it wasn't that long ago that I was right where you are. I know how you feel. I understand having questions and concerns. While our situations are different because I didn't have any foundation of faith to return to, I understand the apprehension that goes along with making big decisions like this and not knowing exactly where to start."

He laughed. "I don't think you were ever as skeptical as me."

"What's important is the end result. And if

you're going back to your faith in God, that's what matters the most."

"Yes, it is." He squeezed her hand and thanked God for bringing Sydney into his life.

NINE

Sydney awoke from an awful nightmare to the bright sun streaming into her room. She gasped when she looked at the clock on the nightstand and saw it was almost noon. She never slept that late. Granted it had been almost 3:00 a.m. before she'd practically willed her body to sleep last night.

She pushed any thoughts about Rick out of her mind and instead focused on the current man in her life—Max. Talk about a major breakthrough. Even through this awful ordeal, God was good. Max's return to faith gave her a morale boost that she desperately needed, given all the danger that surrounded them.

Max was a good man. A loyal and honest man. The experience with Rick had damaged her for what she assumed would be forever, and she'd reconciled those feelings within herself. But that didn't mean she couldn't be friends with Max.

She started to move out of the bed, and her body yelled at her. Her muscles ached, and she looked down and saw the bruises on her arm. A flash of the night before hit her hard, causing her to suck in a quick breath. Once again she felt Rick's strong hands pressing into her arms. She saw his intent to inflict as much agony on her as possible.

I'm not going back there, she told herself. Yes, she might be sore and bruised, but she wasn't going to let that stop her from moving forward. Rick Ward no longer held any power over her.

After she went to the bathroom and took a quick shower, she headed downstairs where she heard voices getting louder.

Elena and Max were having what looked to be a heated discussion. Elena stood with her hands on her hips as she spoke to Max.

Sydney walked into the kitchen. "What's going on, you two?"

Elena immediately stopped talking and turned to her but didn't say anything.

"Come on." She was starting to get frustrated at being locked out of the important discussions. "This all involves me. I think I have a right to know. Was there a problem with the FBI or the marshals?"

Elena shook her head. "No. Everything went

smoothly. The marshals are enacting special security protocols in case Davies isn't the only one involved. They're also looking for Davies. The FBI is assisting."

"That's all good news." Sydney was confused. What was she missing? "If that's all true, then what's the problem between the two of you?"

Silence filled the kitchen and Elena avoided making eye contact with her.

"Max?" she asked.

He let out a breath. "It's the Diaz trial. The court has reset the trial to begin tomorrow."

As she looked into his green eyes, her pulse quickened. "Wait. That doesn't make any sense. Why so fast?"

"Let me explain," Elena said. "After we got done talking to the FBI and marshals first thing this morning, we had a status conference with the judge and the attorneys for both sides. Everyone in that conference agreed that since we now have a much better idea of the threat assessment the trial could proceed. Including your expert testimony against Kevin Diaz."

Sydney turned her attention away from Elena and back to Max. "And let me guess, you are not in favor of me going to the courthouse and testifying tomorrow?"

He took a step toward her. "Of course I'm

not in favor of it. It's far too risky." He paced around the kitchen. Then he turned toward Elena. "Am I the only one who remembers what happened the last time we went into that court-house? Sydney almost got killed! We shouldn't be taking those types of unnecessary risks. I don't care that the players involved think they have a handle on the threat. Because let me tell you, they're wrong. They don't really have any idea of how deep this could go or the power that East River could exert. The damage they could do—will do—if we attempt to restart this trial and put Sydney back up on that witness stand."

"What about that woman who was mur-dered?" Elena said. "She was only in her twen-ties. A teacher with her entire life ahead of her. Without Sydney's testimony, Kevin Diaz will probably be found not guilty by that jury. That victim deserves justice. Are we just going to pretend like her life isn't of value, too?"

"Elena's right." Sydney walked to Max and put her hand on his shoulder to stop him from pacing. "I'm ready to testify. I've been ready to testify and put that behind me. It's my job. I'm an expert witness. It's what I do."

Max shook his head. "It's too dangerous."

"This time we'll be better prepared," Elena said. "Davies won't be able to get in there be-cause everyone now knows about him. There will be plenty of security. Probably more security than you can imagine. The higher-ups in both the FBI and marshals want to clean up their public image, especially after what happened before. I can guarantee you that they will not be stingy with resource allocation on this. I know we can get this done. Ward's picture is being circulated to every law enforcement agency in the state. We're on the attack now. You can't even begin to compare what happened before to our current situation. We have a completely different understanding of the facts on the ground."

"Yeah, but what about all the other East River gang members that we don't know? It's a public trial. Other gang members could easily get inside, and no one would even identify them as a possible threat. What about that?"

"I'm telling you, Max, the security will be airtight," Elena said. Then Elena turned and looked at her. "Ultimately this is your call, Sydney. The prosecution wants you to testify. They retained you as an expert and believe that your testimony is vital to obtaining a murder conviction. But given the circumstances no one is going to go after you for breach of your expert-witness agreement if you back out. I've confirmed that fact with the prosecutor."

Sydney pushed her shoulders back and knew

her answer. "I am not backing out. No way. I'm going to testify against a murderer and help put that man away so he can't harm any other innocent women."

"But, Sydney, I'm already worried about what could have happened to Brian," Max said. "Now you're putting yourself right in the line of fire."

While she was grateful for his concern, she had a job to do. "I understand that you're upset and concerned about Brian. We all are. But I'm sorry, Max. I have to testify."

Max walked out of the room without saying another word, leaving her alone with Elena.

"He'll come around," Elena said. "It'll just take him a little time to get his head wrapped around all of it. Then he'll want to go full in on the details and security preparation. He's just frustrated by his lack of control over everything, and especially the uncertainty looming about Brian."

"I know he means well, but you understand that I have to do this, right?"

Elena smiled. "Yes, I do. And I still don't feel right about what I did with Davies. I know you said that you moved past it, but I can't help but think that was the biggest mistake of my career. One I won't ever be able to put behind me. I appreciate you being understanding, but it was a colossal failure on my part. A lapse in judgment that I can't even really explain."

She grabbed Elena's hand. "I don't want you to think another thought about that. At the time you did what you thought was best. You had no idea how things would spiral out of control. Nor did you know anything about Rick. Like you said earlier, things have changed. We're operating under a different set of circumstances now."

"That means a lot to me. My job is my life, Sydney. And to think that I put you in danger through my actions is antithetical to everything I believe in and stand for."

"We all make mistakes. You're a solid marshal. Don't doubt that."

"Thanks, Sydney. You have both been great in a very difficult and complex situation." Elena smiled and so did Sydney.

Sydney thought that under different circumstances, Elena was someone she easily could call a friend. But they had more pressing matters to attend to now. As if she read her mind, Elena brought them back to the task at hand with another bit of news.

"I did some more digging on Ward's conviction."

"And what did you find?" Sydney asked.

"He did time for robbery. He cut a deal, and it never went to trial. The interesting thing is that there were no witnesses. I think Ward definitely took the fall for someone in East River. I just don't know who or why. But that could be the reason why he and Lucas Jones are so tight now. If Jones asked him to help a fellow gang member, then that would explain why Jones is willing to help him out now with you."

She let out a breath. "And to think this whole thing could all go back to Rick's hatred of me. It's just staggering."

"Max told me how you handled yourself with Rick last night," Elena said with admiration in her dark eyes. "You've proven yourself to be very tough. How long have you been training?"

"For years. I started a couple months after I ran away from him."

Elena reached out and touched her shoulder. "You're a strong woman, Sydney. I admire how you've handled yourself in this very difficult predicament." Elena stopped for a moment and looked away. "Honestly, I don't think I would've been that brave if I had been in your shoes."

"Oh, you would have and then some. It took me a long time to get where I am now. But I'm thankful that I'm stronger and better equipped to take on a man like Rick."

"We're going to catch him, Sydney. That's my promise to you. I may have failed you with regard to Davies, but I won't fail you again. I'll be there at the courthouse. Nothing is going to happen to you."

"I know." And the strange thing was she really believed that.

Max couldn't believe he was back yet again in the courthouse parking lot with Sydney. The last time they had gone in that building it was a near disaster. Why would this be any different?

He was apparently the only one who was concerned about something bad happening. Everyone else was totally on board with Sydney going to the trial and testifying. It was taking a lot of self-discipline to put on a professional face and be a team player when all he really wanted to do was take Sydney out of there and keep her safe from Ward and East River.

"Max?" Sydney asked. "Shouldn't we be going in now?"

Max nodded. He wasn't going to take out his frustration on Sydney. She was just doing what she thought was right. He knew that. His car was parked in the back of the courthouse, and they had a combination of marshals and FBI agents waiting outside to escort them in.

She reached over and squeezed his arm.

"You shouldn't be encouraging me, Syd. It's supposed to be the other way around."

"The way I see it right now we're a team."

He smiled. "Let's keep it that way." Knowing he couldn't stall any longer, he told her, "Wait for me, and I'll come around to your door." He got out of the car and took a deep breath. This was it. The moment he'd been dreading. He walked around to Sydney's side of the car flanked by an agent on each side.

They'd agreed that as part of the stepped up security there would be at least three agents plus Max with Sydney at all times. The last thing they wanted was a repeat of the incident with Davies. Looking back, he realized it hadn't been a smart move to have only the two of them on Sydney. They wouldn't make that mistake again. Max also had handpicked the people who would have access to Sydney—a combination of marshals and FBI agents that would provide that extra layer of security.

After opening the door, he took her arm. Agents were on each side of him plus additional an additional security perimeter.

"Are we going to the same room we were in last time?" she asked.

"No. I didn't want to put you through that. We're going to be in another conference room. Same kind of room, just not the exact one. I thought that would be better for all of us."

"That's fine."

Sydney looked like an expert witness today in a black pantsuit and a light blue blouse with her auburn hair pulled back in a bun. Her slightly flushed cheeks showed a bit of her nerves and excitement. Max knew how much this testimony meant to her.

He guided her to a conference room on the opposite end of the hall. One of the other agents checked the room and yelled "Clear!" before they walked in.

"This is really happening," she said softly as she took a seat.

"Yes, it is." He looked at his watch. "Probably in about fifteen minutes."

She drummed her fingers on the table. Neither Max nor any of the other agents spoke. At this point, he thought, what was there to say? All he cared about was keeping Sydney safe, and so far she was. The sooner she could testify and he could get her out of the courthouse the better.

He'd been adamant that people entering the courtroom be checked a second time for weapons. He wasn't willing to take any chances and with the possibility of human error, he liked doubling up on precautionary measures.

Minutes later, feeling Sydney's tension build, he turned to her. "You ready for your testimony?"

"Yes." She looked at him, her eyes wide, her shoulders squared. "I know you're skeptical about my abilities when it comes to pure sketch art, but I have the utmost confidence in my work."

He held up his hand. "Sydney, my issues were based on one bad experience and shouldn't impact you at all. I don't want you thinking about that before you testify. I never should've even brought up my concerns. If I had to do it all over again, I would've kept my mouth closed on that topic."

"But you didn't."

"You don't have anything to prove to me. I promise you that," he assured her.

But she didn't respond.

About twenty minutes later he was starting to get antsy when there was a knock at the door. One of the agents opened it, and Elena stood on the other side.

"We're ready for her," Elena said.

Max stood up. "You ready, Syd?"

"Definitely. Let's do this."

Sydney was telling the truth. She was ready to testify and get this behind her. She had to keep telling herself to think about this the way she had thought about all her other cases. Not to focus on the security and threats, but to do her job as a professional forensic artist. A job she knew she was good at. She wanted to do her part to send a guilty man to prison for the kidnapping and murder of an innocent woman. A young woman who had had her whole life ahead of her, only to have it stolen by Kevin Diaz. She had been only twenty-five.

Sydney pushed the doubt Max had unwittingly planted from her mind. He'd made those comments before he'd known her that well. But his misgivings about the accuracy of traditional sketch art still played a little tune of insecurity in the back of her head.

Her heels clicked loudly on the floor as she walked down the hall, and she focused on that noise. Blocked everything else out. The walk down the hallway seemed like the length of a football field. She forced herself to breathe and prayed for the strength and wisdom to do her job to the best of her ability.

They reached the courtroom, and she steadied herself as Max squeezed her arm. He was letting her know it would all be okay. He was focusing on her security so she could focus on what she had to do.

One of the other agents pushed open the courtroom door, and they escorted her inside. She looked up and saw the jury was already in their seats. All of their attention was turned to her as she walked down the courtroom aisle.

The judge looked at the prosecutor. "Are you ready, Ms. Lutz?"

"Yes, your honor. The prosecution calls Sydney Berry to the stand."

Sydney walked to the witness stand and sat down.

"Ms. Berry," the judge said. "You were previously sworn in. I know it's been quite a few days, but this is just a reminder that you remain under oath. Do you understand that?"

"Yes, your honor." The judge had gray hair and kind blue eyes. He was known as a stickler for procedure, but he had a reputation for being fair.

"Ms. Berry," the prosecutor began. "Last time we were here we got the preliminaries and your background out of the way that properly established you as an expert witness. Now, I'd like to have you explain to the jury what work you've done on this case specifically."

"Of course. I met with the eyewitness, Ms. Sheila Baker, who provided me with details of the man she saw the night the victim was kidnapped and murdered. Based on that meeting, which lasted about two hours, I generated a sketch." She was careful not to provide any commentary about the actual crime.

That wasn't her area. She was the artist, not the detective.

"Your honor, the prosecution would now move to have the sketch drawn by Ms. Berry entered into evidence," Ms. Lutz said.

"Any objections?" asked the judge.

"We'd like to renew our motion to exclude the sketch," Mr. Pines, the defense attorney, said.

The judge shook his head. "Mr. Pines, I've already ruled on the general admissibility of the sketch produced by Ms. Berry during pretrial hearings."

"Yes, your honor. I remember the expert hearing well where we argued over Ms. Berry's qualifications. But I would still like to respectfully renew the motion to exclude the sketch."

The judge stood firm. "Mr. Pines, if you have objections to raise that are substantively different, then you can make them. Otherwise, the sketch is admitted as state's exhibit twenty-two."

"No, your honor. I don't have anything new." Mr. Pines looked down and took a seat.

Sydney had been a part of the protracted pretrial hearing months ago on the admissibility of her sketch as part of her qualifications to testify as an expert. At the end of the day, the prosecution had won that argument which would allow her to testify as an expert witness in the case.

"Thank you, your honor," Ms. Lutz said. "I'd like the sketch to be published to the jury now, via the monitor."

Sydney's sketch went up on the big screen for the entire jury to see. Ms. Lutz was a seasoned prosecutor. She knew exactly what she was doing. She purposely gave the jury a minute to digest the sketch before she continued her examination.

Even Sydney herself couldn't believe how spot on the sketch was. There was no doubt that the man in the sketch was the defendant, Kevin Diaz. And by the looks on the jurors' faces they were thinking the same thing. Several jurors sat wide-eyed while others looked back and forth between the big screen and the defendant.

Sydney performed very well during the rest of Ms. Lutz's questions but that was to be expected since she was a witness for the state and they'd had extensive meetings to prepare for her testimony. But now it was the defense's turn, and she knew Mr. Pines wasn't going to hold back. No, he was going to try to destroy her.

Mr. Pines walked toward her, never breaking eye contact. It was his first step in attempting to intimidate her. "Isn't it true, Ms. Berry, that as a sketch artist you actually come up with faces that you draw based on what people tell you?"

The defense attorney stared her down, daring her to deny his statement. But she wasn't afraid. The truth was on her side.

"Mr. Pines, you are correct that I'm a sketch artist, but you're wrong in your characterization that I *come up with* the faces I draw. My sketches are based solely on information provided by the witnesses. Very specific information. They're not something I create based on my own whims or imagination."

Mr. Pines let silence fall over the courtroom. He was in his fifties, a seasoned defense attorney. One of the best around. And Kevin Diaz had paid big bucks for his services.

It bothered her that she felt as though Max probably would agree with Mr. Pines about her work as a sketch artist. But for now she had to put that out of her mind.

Mr. Pines turned in a dramatic fashion, waving his right arm around as he looked toward the jury with his big dark eyes and then back at her. "Ms. Berry, now let's not be disingenuous to this hardworking jury."

"Objection, your honor." Ms. Lutz the prosecutor stood up. "Improper commentary about the jury."

"Sustained," the judge said. "The jury is instructed to disregard the last comment made by Mr. Pines."

"Isn't it very possible, Ms. Berry, that you saw Mr. Diaz in the news the week before you met with the eyewitness and that you subconsciously used him in that sketch when the witness happened to bring up similar features?"

Sydney was ready for this. She'd had her deposition taken months ago and had told the truth then, as she would now. That she had in fact seen Kevin Diaz before. But she was firm in her position that seeing him in passing on the news a week before she met with the witness had nothing to do with her sketch. Diaz had been interviewed about his latest construction project that was supposed to bring millions into the city, and he'd done multiple local TV news interviews.

Before she could answer, the defense attorney kept going. "And since you filled in those blanks with a similar-looking man that you could use as a point of reference, you're now asking the jury to convict an innocent man?"

"No," she said quietly. "That's not true." She didn't know why she didn't respond more loudly.

"You're under oath, Ms. Berry." His voice rang out loudly, and he pounded the podium.

She flinched at his show of force.

"Can you say, under oath, that you are one hundred percent certain that seeing Mr. Diaz in the news only days before you met with the witness didn't impact your drawing?"

"It did not." She felt her composure slipping. He was calling into question her integrity.

"And you're sure?"

"Mr. Pines, I think I've answered your question." Right after she said those words, she wanted to take them back. She sounded too defensive, and that was not how she wanted to project herself to the jury.

"How can you be so certain?"

She sat up taller in the witness chair. "Because I'm telling you the truth, and I'm certain that seeing Mr. Diaz on the local news didn't impact me at all." She tried to keep her voice steady, but she was faltering. Pines smelled blood and was going in for the kill. Why was she letting him get inside her head? She never should've let Max's opinion get to her.

"You don't sound too convinced to me," the attorney said. "But I know you don't want your professional credibility called into question for the whole world to see. That would definitely impact your ability to keep getting hired as an expert witness now, wouldn't it, Ms. Berry?"

"Objection, he's badgering the witness, your honor," Ms. Lutz said.

"I'll withdraw." Mr. Pines took a step back. "That's all I have for now."

Sydney tried to calm her breathing, though she was having a hard time. Pines had sown the seeds of doubt. And that was all he needed as a defense attorney. Reasonable doubt.

"Redirect, your honor," Ms. Lutz said as she stood up.

Good, Sydney thought. The prosecutor was going to attempt to clean this up.

"Ms. Berry, at the time you met with the witness, what did you know about Mr. Diaz?"

"Just that he was a successful businessman and quite active in the local community."

"And when you're drawing based upon a witness interview, do you ever think about people you know or famous people and use them as a guide for your sketch?"

"Never."

"Are you sure about that?"

"Quite sure, Ms. Lutz. I am confident that I drew that sketch based purely on the information given to me by the witness, and not on any outside influence of any kind."

"That's all I have for the witness, your honor."

"You're dismissed, Ms. Berry."

As Sydney stepped down off the stand, she wondered if the prosecution's redirect would be enough, but she feared it was not going to be. The defense had rattled her and put a plausible alternative theory into the jury's mind.

The prosecution would want to use her sketch to strengthen the testimony of the eyewitness. Since eyewitnesses could often be discredited, having the sketch as a contemporaneous piece of evidence was critical to the state's case.

She heard the judge speaking as Max and the other agents escorted her to the door. "I understand that was the final witness. Closing statements to start in thirty minutes."

Sydney's stomach clenched as she realized it was entirely possible that a verdict could come down as soon as today.

Max's strong arm steadied her as they walked out of the courtroom and down the hallway.

"You did great," he said.

She kept her eyes straight ahead as she retorted, "Don't patronize me, Max. There's definitely reasonable doubt planted by Mr. Pines." She felt sick knowing that a killer could be set free. "I was honest. If I wouldn't have been so honest in my deposition, this wouldn't have even been an issue."

"But you were honest as you should've been. You did everything you could, Syd. It's completely out of your hands now. Let the jury do its job."

She looked at him then. "So you're trying to tell me that given your preconceptions about sketch artists, you would convict based on my testimony?"

"There are a lot of factors that would go into my decision."

She felt anger bubbling beneath the surface. She needed to take a deep breath before they got into a useless argument.

They walked out of the courthouse surrounded by security. "What's next now?" she asked.

"I'll explain once we're secure at the FBI safe house."

She didn't like the sound of that one bit.

TEN

Finally, they were alone at the safe house. Or at least alone for the moment. Elena was outside making phone calls. Max knew what he had to do now. He took a deep breath as he grabbed Sydney's hand and led her into the living room.

"There's something you don't want to tell me," Sydney said, correctly gauging his mood.

"Have a seat on the couch with me," he said. He'd gone over different strategies in his head of how to handle this. But at the end of the day he just needed to be direct and honest. That was what Sydney would expect from him, and it was what she deserved.

"I'm listening." She sat down beside him and held his hand. "Whatever it is, Max, I promise you I can handle it. Is this about my testimony?"

He ran his left hand through his hair. "No, it's not about that. There are some security issues and disputes revolving around you."

"What do you mean? What kind of disputes?"

"Well, the people above Elena at the marshals believe that your security situation is completely tied up with Ward. They don't think you're under any threat from Kevin Diaz."

"That could be true," she said. "At the beginning of all this, we didn't know that Rick was in the picture. All we know for certain now is the connection between Rick and East River."

He nodded. "But you see, the problem is that the marshals are ready to cut you lose."

Her eyes widened. "Cut me loose? What are you talking about?"

"Meaning no more security detail. They definitely don't think there's any basis for entry into the witness-protection program at this point. The way they see it, this is a domestic dispute. A very dangerous one, but one that falls outside of their mission and jurisdiction."

She didn't say anything for a minute. And he gave her time to process it. "So what does this mean for me now? Do I just go back to my regular life?"

"I don't want you to do that. You're still in danger."

"Then what would you have me do?"

Here it was. She wasn't going to like this, but he wanted to do it. "I'm going to take leave and provide you with security on my own." He paused. "If you'll allow it."

She shook her head. "No, you can't just leave your job indefinitely and follow me around."

"I don't look at it at all like that, Syd. You're still in danger."

She stood and walked a couple of steps away from the sofa before turning back to him. "Don't you get it? As long as Rick Ward is free, I'm in danger. That could be the rest of my life."

"The FBI is going to do their best to catch Ward. It's only a matter of time. The FBI gang unit still cares a lot about him and Lucas Jones and whatever else East River is up to."

"But the FBI doesn't really have an interest in my security," she said matter-of-factly.

"It's more of a resources issue. If there's a specific threat, then the FBI will probably act on your behalf."

"You mean if there are *more* specific threats. I've already been threatened."

He detected the change in her tone, could feel her hackles go up. "I'm on your side here, Syd. Which is why I want you to let me help you get through this. Let the FBI focus on catching Ward with evidence that will stick."

"So you're just what? Going to put your entire life on hold for me? What's in it for you?"

"You should know me better than that by now." He reached out and gently took her hand. "I care about you, Sydney. Spending more time with you definitely won't be a hardship."

"I'll agree to this on one condition."

The look in her eyes let him know that he was probably going to hate her condition. "What is it?"

"That we use me to set a trap for Rick. We catch him and have him put away once and for all. That way we can all return to our normal lives."

He didn't want to return to a normal life if Sydney was no longer in it. "I don't like putting you in more danger than you already are."

"I agree, but you know it's a good idea. We can flush him out. This is the best way, not having the FBI running around aimlessly searching for him."

"There's just one problem with your plan."

"And what's that?"

"If we use you to draw Ward out, you will be directly in harm's way. And I'm not just going to sit back and hand you over to your ex. He's hurt you once under my care, and I'm not going to let that happen again."

She looked away from him and bit her bottom lip. "We can figure out something that will work. Don't give up on the idea just yet."

Max was about to object when Elena walked into the living room, her lips drawn downward into a tight frown.

"The verdict is in," she announced.

Sydney took a step toward Elena. "What was it?"

"I'm sorry, Sydney. The jury found Diaz not guilty."

Sydney collapsed on the sofa and put her head in her hands. Tears ran down her cheeks. "I failed," she said.

Elena walked over and patted her on the shoulder, whispering something in her ear. Then she stood up. "I'll give you two a minute."

When Sydney looked up at him with tears in those big brown eyes, he felt as though someone had punched him in the gut. Without hesitation he walked to the sofa, sat down beside her and wrapped his arm around her. "I'm here, Syd. Let it out."

Neither of them said a word for a long time. Finally, she looked up at him. "Are you happy now? Everything you said about sketch artists appears to be true. The jury must've all thought like you."

He pulled his arm back. "I never criticized your work, Syd. You are a talented artist. And my issues with traditional sketch artists have nothing to do with you. I told you I made hasty generalizations based on one bad experience."

She pushed up from the sofa. "Max, I did everything wrong. My job is to provide expert testimony. Credible and professional testimony. And I failed. The jury obviously believed that seeing Kevin Diaz on the news somehow influenced my drawing. In this instance, the fact that the sketch so closely resembled the defendant worked against me. The jury didn't believe I was skilled enough to draw that accurately based on witness statements alone. They had to have thought that I was basing it on outside influences."

"You're not at fault, Sydney. You're great at your job. You know how difficult criminal convictions are. Beyond a reasonable doubt—that's our justice system. You can't let this impact how you feel about your professional abilities. And you should give yourself a bit of a break. You didn't exactly testify under normal circumstances, you know. There have been multiple attempts on your life."

His words obviously didn't get through to her because she quickly replied, "How would you feel in my shoes? I know how seriously you take your job. So just sit back for a minute and think about that."

She was hurting, and it killed him that he

couldn't provide her with the comfort she needed. When he reached out to her, she pulled back.

"I'd like some time alone." She took a step back and walked away.

He refused to let this erect a wall between them. Not after everything they'd been through together. He'd give her a little time to process it. But he definitely wasn't letting her go. He desperately wanted to be able to go back to their conversation in that diner and take back his comments about the reliability of sketch artists. She'd not been at the top of her game today, and it wasn't her fault. It was his. And that fact ate at him.

Sydney let the tears flow freely once she was alone in the bedroom. Because of her lackluster testimony, a murderer was now free. Back to his millions of dollars, fancy cars and his highly esteemed position in the community.

She had to give it to Mr. Pines. He'd done his job. Much better than she had done hers. She replayed the cross examination over and over in her head. What could she have said differently? More emphatically? What about her body language? Had the jury just not wanted to believe that a popular businessman could be capable of such a heinous crime?

She beat herself up because she hadn't performed at the level she expected of herself. She'd let the defense attorney shake her, and once the jury had seen that tiny flicker of uncertainty it had been good enough to create reasonable doubt.

It didn't help that she felt a bit sour toward Max. Even though she knew rationally she shouldn't, he'd been the one to start sowing the seeds of doubt in her mind. Then Mr. Pines had come in for the kill.

And now she felt utterly helpless. There was nothing she could do. Diaz couldn't be tried again for this crime because of double jeopardy. She could only pray he wouldn't kill again. But she'd done enough research in criminology to know that he likely would. Especially a powerful and egotistical man like he was. He'd gotten away with murder, so why not do it again? The thought sickened her.

She let out a sigh. So where did she go from here? Her thoughts went back to Max. Back to his proposition to serve as her personal bodyguard. She'd been serious about her condition. Unless they were affirmatively going to try to catch Rick, she wasn't going to let Max waste his career following her around each day. A battle with Rick could last a lifetime—until one of them got killed in the process.

Max probably had the wrong impression

about the life she lived. The past couple of weeks had been frightening and dangerous, but normally her days were quiet. Yes, she met with witnesses regularly, but she didn't testify each week. Maybe once every couple months, if that often, and only in the major cases. Most of her work was performed quietly with local police or FBI and providing sketches to help them find the perpetrator.

She wondered if she'd have the nerve to get back onto the witness stand again. Failure was something she didn't handle well, and there was no way around it this time. She had failed. She could try to blame Max or Mr. Pines, but the fault rested solely on her shoulders.

Pushing that awful thought out of her mind, she got up from the bed and looked out the second floor window. Elena and Max were below her talking on the front steps—no doubt about what they were going to do with her.

What she really wanted to do was go home. Try to forget the past few days entirely. But she knew it was never that easy. *Lord, please give me the strength to get through this.* She paused in her prayer. *And, Lord, please guide me in what I need to do with Max.* She meant not only with regard to her protection but on a personal level, as well. A fresh wave of tears streamed down her cheeks.

She needed to get some air. She walked downstairs and out on to the front porch. Elena and Max turned to look at her.

"I'd like to take a walk," she said. "I need to get out of the house."

"I'll go with you," Max said quickly.

"I'm going to head out." Elena walked over to her and put her hands on Sydney's shoulders. "We'll figure this all out," she said.

Sydney nodded, then Elena left the safe house.

"You ready?" Max asked.

"Yes, I just thought a walk would be nice. I'm tired of feeling so cramped up."

They started walking down the neighborhood sidewalk lit only by dim streetlights. Beside her, she knew Max was alert.

"What were you and Elena talking about?" she asked him.

He hesitated, only a second, but she detected his reluctance and looked at him. "The local police found Brian," he said.

"Oh, no!" She assumed the worst.

"He was on the side of the interstate. He's alive but has been badly beaten. He's been hospitalized."

"I'm so sorry. That happened because of me."

"It wasn't your fault. It was Ward and East River who are responsible."

Max could tell her that all night, but it was difficult for her to accept. "What are Elena's current thoughts on my situation?"

"She agrees that you're still at risk from Ward and East River. But her hands are tied. Her bosses have made the decision. The US Marshals' assignment is over."

"Have you given any more thought to what I said about getting Rick put away once and for all?"

"I'm still thinking about it." He grabbed her hand as they walked.

This time she didn't pull away and enjoyed the warmth of his hand in hers. "In the meantime, where do we go from here?"

"I'm not leaving your side, that's where. Tom has secured us use of the safe house for one week. That's all he can do from the FBI side. So we need a plan for what to do after that."

"Why can't we just go back to our lives?"

"We've been over that. I can't let you just go on as if nothing has happened. And I surely can't just go back to my job knowing you're in danger."

"But that's what you signed up for, Max. You're a US marshal now. You protect witnesses and those in the witness protection program. I'm neither at this point."

He stopped walking and turned her to face

him. "Sydney, I hear exactly what you're saying. But since I met you none of the things that used to matter seem to matter quite as much as you do. Especially if it's a life without you in it."

"What are you saying?"

"I'm saying that I've really grown to care about you. And nothing will stand in the way of me protecting you. Not because it's my job or out of some sense of professional duty. But because I want you in my life. I want you to be safe. I need you to be safe."

Emotions flushed through her. To hear Max say those words frightened her. Because she didn't know if she could ever open up to a man again. To trust and to love. Even if the man was Max. Someone she'd actually started to trust. But she'd been fighting her way back from vulnerability. And while Max and Rick were nothing alike, she still dealt with the emotional pain of what Rick had done to her. Those scars were as bad as the physical ones. "Max, I don't even know what to say." She leaned into him, and he wrapped his arm tightly around her shoulder. "Max, you've been a great friend to me. But I also refuse to be the reason you throw away your career."

He pulled back and looked her directly in the

eyes. "I'm not throwing away my career. And your safety is more important."

This man really cared about her. She wasn't used to such compassion. "You're not the same man you were when I met you a short time ago."

He nodded. "You can say that again. Syd, you've made me start to question everything. My career, my goals, my beliefs. And in the best possible way."

"Really?" She didn't know how to take that. "Yes."

"You seemed so set in your ways at the beginning," she said. "What changed?"

"Knowing you. Seeing how you live. Your strength and courage. Your faith. I can't really describe it very well. In fact, I still have a long way to go. But you make me want to keep changing. To not be so cynical about life. There are so many thoughts bouncing around in my head."

She was blown away by Max's characterization of how she had impacted his life. "Can I ask you something?"

"Sure. I've asked you enough questions since we've known each other."

"My past has been on display because of the situation with Rick. But I don't know anything about yours. Why aren't you with someone?

You've got a wonderful career. You're smart, funny and handsome."

He smiled. "Hey, now you're going to embarrass me."

"I'm serious, though. It doesn't make a lot of sense to me that you're alone. Why don't you have someone special in your life?"

"Honestly, my job has been priority number one. And two and three and four. You get the picture. I've casually dated, but most women aren't happy about my erratic schedule, the long hours, the broken dates. I've been a pretty absent boyfriend. And women don't like that very much. But I really didn't care enough about investing myself in a relationship to really push the issue. Also, we've talked about the way I was raised. Showing emotion and trusting in someone else is not something I do easily—or really at all."

She had just opened her mouth to respond when a car came barreling down the street headed straight at them.

ELEVEN

Max didn't hesitate as he lunged toward Sydney, pushing her hard and far out of the way of the oncoming gray SUV. He covered her body with his as he heard gunshots.

God, please help us right now. More gunshots rang out in rapid succession. When he felt a bullet slice through his skin, he was just thankful it was him and not Sydney who'd been hit.

He felt her shaking underneath him as the squeal of the tires indicated the SUV was driving away quickly.

"You're bleeding!" she gasped. Her eyes were wide with fear, and she gripped him tightly.

"It's just a graze." At least that's what he hoped. "Are you okay?"

"Yes. Thanks to you."

As he lifted himself off her a burning pain shot through his left arm. "We need to get back to the house."

"You're losing a lot of blood. Can you walk?" she asked.

"Yes." He grimaced.

She grabbed on to him. "Here, lean on me."

He put his right arm around her, more to convince himself she was unharmed than for the support.

He scanned the street as they walked quickly back to the house. He didn't think the truck would return, but he couldn't, wouldn't, take a chance.

"I guess we know who was behind that," she said.

"Yeah. I don't know if Rick Ward was the one taking the shots, but I'm certain he was the one calling them."

By the time they entered the house, his arm was burning as if it was on fire and his breathing was becoming labored.

"I've got to make sure the bleeding is stopped," she said, helping him to the couch. "Are you able to remove your dress shirt?"

"I'll try." With each movement the pain got worse. He tried to stay focused.

She pulled the sleeve off his arm. It had become stuck because of the blood. His T-shirt was also covered in blood.

She gasped when she saw the wound. "This looks bad, Max."

"I thought it was just a knick."

"That's the biggest and bloodiest knick I've ever seen."

"The bullet didn't go into me, though." He pressed down hard on the wound with his already destroyed dress shirt.

"I think you need to go to the hospital and have this checked out."

Gingerly, he pulled his phone out of the hip holster. "Tom," he said. "I need medical attention at the safe house. Can you send someone?"

"What's going on?"

He filled Tom in on the shooting and his injury. "We're having a hard time stopping the bleeding. I might need some help to get it stopped and stitched up."

"I'll bring someone now and then move you to another location. I knew there was too much in and out at that safe house. They probably followed Elena or one of my people at some point."

"Thanks, Tom. I know you don't have to do this."

"Max, I promised you a safe house for a week, and I'm staying true to that. Just hang tight."

"See you soon." He hung up the phone and looked at Sydney who was walking back into the room with a wet towel to clean him up.

"What did he say?"

"He's on his way and bringing medical help. Then he's going to get us to a new house. It's not safe here any longer."

She gently touched the wet towel to his wound. He tried not to flinch. Thankfully, he had been hit in his left arm. He could shoot with both hands, but he was a much better shot right handed.

"I'm sorry," she said.

"No, you're doing the right thing. If anything, you need to get a fresh dry towel to apply more pressure to help stop the bleeding."

"I don't want to hurt you."

He grinned. "I can handle it."

When she swapped out the towel and pushed down hard on his arm, he thought he might pass out from the pain. But he had to stay strong for her. "Talk to me to keep my mind off it."

"How do you think they found us in this neighborhood?"

"Tom thinks we had too many people coming and going over past couple of days. He and Elena could've been followed even, if not to the house, to the neighborhood in general. I know they were being careful, but professional tails can be very difficult to detect."

"It all happened so fast. One moment we were having this nice conversation, and the next I saw the SUV coming toward us. I knew right then and there that Rick was coming for me again." He detected a slight tremor in her voice and knew she was trying hard to hold it together. "How did you react so quickly?"

"I think it was just instinct. I wanted to protect you. And in that moment, Syd, I prayed. I prayed hard for God to protect us both."

"And He certainly did." She looked at Max then and took his right hand in hers. Her touch was warm, comforting. "Don't worry about me. I'm fine. I'm more worried about you and your injury. You've lost a bit of blood. I'm thankful that it wasn't worse, though."

The door slammed shut and Tom and another guy who looked like an FBI medic came into the room.

"How're you doing?" Tom asked.

"It hurts like crazy," Max told him. "But at least the bleeding is under control somewhat."

Tom introduced the medic he'd brought. "This is Simon Lang. He'll take a look at you."

The medic reached into his bag. "I'll give you something for the pain, but it's going to take a few minutes to kick in. So it may hurt for a bit as I examine you."

Simon was right. Once he started stitching, Max succumbed to the pain. He closed his eyes and passed out.

* * *

Sydney looked down at Max lying in the bed at the new safe house. The FBI medic had given him something stronger after he and Tom had helped transport them to the new safe house. Tom was still downstairs waiting for Max to wake up.

Sydney squeezed Max's hand. She hoped that he could feel, even if only subconsciously, that she was beside him—supporting him in whatever way he needed.

When he had told her about what happened before the accident and how he'd prayed, she had felt blessed. "Lord, You really do work in mysterious ways," she whispered.

She was more convinced than ever of God's hand in this entire journey, as they once again had come out of a perilous experience alive. Even through the evil and danger coming at her from Rick and East River, she had peace, because she believed that all things worked together for good as long as you had faith in God.

While she had hoped she would never see Rick again, she was assured by her faith that God had a plan.

"Hey."

She looked down at Max and saw his eyes opening slowly. "Hey."

"What in the world happened?"

"You passed out from the pain before the pain meds really kicked in. Then the medic gave you another injection once we were transported here."

"So we're in the new safe house?"

"Yes."

"Alone?"

"No. Tom is waiting downstairs. He said he didn't want to leave while you were still knocked out."

"He's really been great through this whole thing."

She concurred. "Did you work with him much while you were at the FBI?"

"Only about six months, but he and Brian actually worked together on a special team years ago and then again more recently." He shook his head. "I need to get up. And since we're talking about Brian, I assume Tom didn't give you any further updates."

"No. Just that he's still in the hospital. No change in his condition. Still critical."

Max sat up and slowly slid his legs off the bed.

"Are you sure you shouldn't stay in bed for a bit longer?"

"No. I want to talk to Tom."

"Let me help you downstairs."

"You seem to be helping me a lot lately, Syd. It's supposed to be the other way around."

"We're a team, remember?"

He smiled. "Yes, I remember." He paused. "Let's go."

She helped him down the stairs about half-way until Tom heard them and came and took over.

"You should be resting, Max," Tom said.

"You've been here long enough. I didn't want to keep you later tonight than you had to be." He sat on the sofa. "Any updates on Brian?"

"He's critical but stable," Tom said as he sat across from him. "He's in an induced coma to try to help the swelling on the brain go down. We'll have to see how that goes."

Sydney saw the concern on Max's face for his friend. "Why can't Rick and Davies be pros-ecuted for what they did to Brian?" she asked.

"We're working on it, but right now the evi-dence is sparse, and without Brian's testimony we don't really know what to look for," Tom said.

"But you won't give up on that, right?" Syd-ney needed to keep up hope.

"Of course not, Sydney. Brian's one of my own men. I want this to stick as much as any-one."

"Thanks," she said.

"I did hear that there were protests outside the courthouse after the verdict was read. For whatever that's worth to you. I know you wanted a different result."

She nodded. "I could've done more. I should've done more."

"From where I sit, you did everything in your power as an expert witness."

She didn't believe it, but it was nice of him to say. "Thanks, Tom."

"So the way I see it, there are multiple angles here that we're working against Rick Ward and Phil Davies and trying to connect the two of them. We have the attack on Brian, the shooting today."

"And no concrete evidence yet tying them to either," Max said.

"We'll get it. The Marshals still want to go by the book in investigating one of their own, so they are being cautious in their approach."

"I don't like it," Max said. "But I understand the mentality about not wanting to go too aggressive on one of your own people in case you're wrong. But everyone knows at this point that Ward is bad news.

Hearing that, Sydney couldn't remain quiet. "I don't like just waiting around like a sitting duck. We can't run forever. What happened today only proves that," she said. "Max, I know you don't want to hear this, but we need to consider my idea."

"What's your idea?" Tom asked.

"Using me as bait to capture Rick. And hopefully Davies, too, for that matter."

Tom whistled. "That's dangerous business, Sydney."

She looked into his eyes. "And what happened today wasn't dangerous? Max was shot. We could've been killed. I know Rick better than most. He won't stop until he gets his revenge. Now that he's had a taste of it, he will keep going until he's tracked me down. Even if it's not today or tomorrow or even next week. It could be next year, but he'll find me. The only way for me to be safe is for him to be in prison."

"I take it, Max, that you're against this idea?" Tom asked.

"I am against it, but I also hear what Sydney's saying. If we could do it in a way to minimize the risk to her…"

"Let me give it some thought," Tom said. "I know I'm an old geezer, but I understand how these guys operate. Been doing this for almost forty years."

"Sleep on it, Tom. It's getting late. We'll regroup tomorrow."

"Will do. Are you sure you're okay here alone with Sydney?"

"Yes. My shooting arm is still good. And I think we'll be fine here, at least for the night, anyway."

"I'll come by in the morning and check in." Tom walked out the front door, leaving them alone.

"You should get back in bed and rest," Sydney told Max. "I'll fix something for you to eat. There's plenty of food in the house."

"I'm wide-awake now. The pain medication has worn off." He grimaced as he moved his left arm.

"That's why you should rest. Lie down and I'll bring you something to eat in a few minutes. You need food to get your full strength back."

"I promise you I'm fine. I'm capable of sitting down and eating at the table."

She started to protest, but he held up his hand.

"I'll go back and get in bed after I've eaten. Is that a fair deal?"

"Yes." She got to work fixing soup and grilled cheese sandwiches. It wasn't until she'd smelled it that she realized she hadn't eaten, either. Her stomach rumbled.

Max's phone rang then, and he picked it up. She could only hear his side of the conversation.

"He's awake?" Max asked.

After some silence and a few words, he hung up.

"Brian?" she asked.

"Yes. The good news is that he's awake. The bad news is that he's suffered some memory loss. The doctors don't know if it will be temporary or permanent. It's common for bad concussions, so we'll have to wait and see. He can't remember anything related to that meeting with Ward."

"Maybe it will come back to him with time." She placed the food on the table. "But I just thank God that he's alive. That's more important than anything else at this point."

He reached out and squeezed her hand. "We're going to get him, Syd. I promise you that. In his quest for revenge, he's being too bold. He'll get sloppy and do something careless."

"I still think we need to talk about my idea."

He took a bite of his sandwich. "I'm listening. How exactly do you propose to use yourself as bait?"

She bit her bottom lip. "Well, that's the thing. I haven't come up with an airtight plan yet. But if I draw him out so that he can be arrested for the assault against me, I'm sure a case can be built against him for his other crimes with enough time to do a thorough investigation. Right now he's gone dark. I'm the best way to get him to reemerge from hiding."

Max frowned. "I see. And how exactly is that going to work without putting you at risk?"

"We'd allow him to get close to me. But the team would be in place to apprehend him before he was able to do any harm to me."

"Do you realize how many things could go wrong in that plan?" He finished off the last bite of his grilled cheese and leaned forward.

"I know there's a risk. But I assume that there would be some type of surveillance on me the entire time. Law enforcement would then capture Rick before anything really happens."

"And what if something goes wrong with the surveillance team? What if you're separated somehow? Then no one will know where you are and you'd be good as dead."

She offered up her best idea. "What if I wore a tracker?"

"You watch too much TV, Syd. If Ward has any sense, the first thing he'd do is search you and all your belongings."

"What if we put it under my skin?"

"Are you crazy?"

"No, I'm serious. I've seen that done on TV

shows, but it can be done in real life, too. Right? There's no way Rick would think I'd do something like that."

"You're right. I think I do need to lie down. I'm not feeling that well."

"You're just trying to avoid confrontation over this."

"I don't want to argue right now, Syd. Let's get some rest and talk about it with Tom in the morning."

She didn't want to relent, but she did, anyway. Mainly because he was injured. And the fact that he was fighting back so hard let her know she was on to something.

Max awoke to voices. He jumped out of the bed and groaned at the pain that shot down his left arm. It was then he realized that the voices belonged to Tom and Sydney.

He took a deep breath to compose himself and walked down the stairs. They were seated at the kitchen table deep in conversation and drinking coffee.

"Good morning," she said. "How're you feeling?"

"Sore, but I'll make it. You should've woken me up when Tom arrived."

"I haven't been here that long," Tom said.

"Sydney was just catching me up on the conversation the two of you had last night."

"Yeah, about that," Max began. "I think I was a bit too foggy from the pain medication to even consider it."

"I think she's got a good idea." Tom took a sip of coffee.

Max couldn't believe he'd heard that. "It's far too dangerous."

But Tom defended his position. "She's right, you know. We can implant a tracker just under her skin. Won't be any big deal and that way there's no way we can lose her."

Max shook his head. "No, the only way we're certain we won't lose her is if we don't allow her to be taken in the first place." He ran a hand through his hair. "This is far too risky to put her out there like this."

"I've thought about it," Tom said. "All we need to do is to be able to catch him. We have Sydney's testimony from the assault against her the other night. That's enough for an assault charge. And hopefully Brian will regain his memory soon, as well."

"So your plan would just have Sydney be used to lure him out but catch him before he takes her."

"Exactly."

"Then why does she need the tracker?"

"Just in case anything goes wrong. It's purely an insurance policy—an extra layer of precaution. The plan would be to apprehend Ward and anyone else with him when he makes the move on Sydney. We'll have a team in range."

"But the team can't be so close as to tip off Ward."

Tom laughed. "This isn't my first rodeo, Max."

"Any ideas on what would be the best type of location?" Sydney asked.

"We would need to think about that." Tom replied.

Max paced around the kitchen for a minute. He knew when he was beat. But if he was going to participate, it had to be run his way. That was the only way to protect Sydney.

"This can't be a one-time operation. Ward will know something is going on if we just send Sydney out by herself. We need to ease into it. The Marshal presence is already gone except for me. The FBI presence needs to go away, too. Then it will just be Sydney and me. We have to make them believe that we're all going back to our normal lives. Rick will just assume Sydney and I have developed a relationship and that's why I'm around. Then after that is set up, Sydney can start going places by herself. But we will need to have an operation plan for each outing. Eventually he'll pounce."

"This will take some planning," Tom said. "And a bit of resources."

"Do you have a better idea?" Max asked him.

"Not really, but I'll keep thinking."

"It's not like you'll need a lot of people," Sydney said.

"No, not many, but it's a commitment over time. At least a few days," Max said. "But if we want this to work, and for you to be safe, then we need to do it right. And that means having the appropriate FBI surveillance and backup team in place."

"I'll authorize the resources, but if we don't have anything after three days, then we'll need to reassess."

"I need you to handpick the agents, Tom. They have to be people you can trust with this."

"Believe me, I fully understand the ramifications. One of my own guys is still laid up in the hospital bed."

Max winced. "I didn't mean it like that, sir. Sorry, I overstepped."

"No, no. Don't worry about it. I know you've been through a lot." Then Tom looked at Sydney. "And you've been through the most. I'll do everything I can to catch Ward and Davies and whoever else in East River might be involved."

"Thank you," Sydney said.

"I'll go get the agents picked out and come up with a general plan of attack. Be ready to leave the house this afternoon."

"Thanks, Tom," Max said.

"I'll be in touch soon." Tom started to walk out of the kitchen when his phone rang. He answered it. After a second of listening, he said. "Are you sure?"

"What's going on?" Sydney asked Max.

"We'll have to wait until he gets off the phone and see."

Tom ended the call and turned back to them. "We've got ourselves a dead body."

TWELVE

Sydney's heartbeat raced. "Who's dead?"

Tom looked down and then back up. "They think it's Davies."

"Davies?" Max asked. "How?"

"I'm about to go find out. I'm meeting representatives from the Marshals on the scene."

"Where?" Max asked.

"A jogger found him on one of the trails in Riverside Park inside the city."

"Wow," Sydney said.

"Yeah, I'm not sure what all of this means, but I'll keep you two posted. We may have to delay our plan for a bit. Just hang tight here while I figure out what's going on. We need to determine how Davies was killed."

Tom walked out the front door, and Sydney turned to Max. "You're thinking something."

"Yeah. I'm thinking that I don't like any of this. I've got a sinking feeling that we're missing something important."

"Like what?" She walked over to where he stood.

"I don't know."

"Come sit with me for a minute." She took his hand and guided him to the couch.

"I have so many thoughts going through my head right now," he said.

She nodded. "I feel the same way. But we can only do what we can from here right now."

"I'd like to go see Brian at some point, but I'm not going to risk it. We'll wait until your security situation gets resolved."

"If it gets resolved."

"It will, Syd."

Did she dare to believe him?

His eyes seemed to darken a shade as he spoke next. "Once this is all over, I want you to give us a shot."

"What do you mean?"

"I hope that we can see each other like normal people do. Go out to dinner, watch a baseball game, that kind of thing."

She wanted nothing more than that, too. But she wondered if it could ever happen. "We're a good match as friends, Max. But once this is all over, I think you'll realize that in the real world we'll never work as a couple."

"But why?"

"I still don't think I'm ready for that. Not just with you, but anyone."

"Don't you think I have my own baggage, too? The fact that I can even consider asking you this is a huge step for me."

"And I appreciate that it's difficult for you, too."

"But?"

"There's also your reservations about my career as a sketch artist."

"I don't question your career." He pulled his hand back and ran it through his hair. "Look, in a perfect world do I prefer scientific approaches to law enforcement? Yes. But we don't live in a perfect world. Watching you testify against Kevin Diaz really showed me what a true expert sketch artist was like."

"Even with the bad result?"

"The jurors made their decision, but that wasn't a reflection on you. Can't you accept my apology about what I said when we first met?"

"I can, but I just I don't know, Max. I don't want to mess up one of the only true friendships I have." Her heart was filled with excitement and trepidation over her feelings for Max. But the dark cloud hanging over everything had to be resolved before she could even entertain any thoughts about a relationship with Max. "Can we table this for now? We've got a lot ahead of us. Let's get through that first. All right?"

She saw the reluctance on his face, but after a moment he nodded. "That's fair."

"I just want to be free of that man, Max. Anything I can do to make that happen once and for all is worth it. I'm willing to take some risks. And you heard Tom today. His idea of the operation would be for me never to get taken by Rick in the first place. Just to be there to help the FBI apprehend him."

"And I hear all of that. I'm sorry. I just can't adequately express my apprehension about all of this. I don't want something to happen to you. I don't think I'd be able to have that on my conscience."

"But don't you see, Max?" She looked up into his big green eyes. "I have to do this. I *need* to do this in order to move on with my life. And I'm frankly ashamed that I was ever with a man like Rick. I don't want you to think less of me because of that. I'm a different person now."

"I would never think less of you because of that. We all make mistakes, Syd."

"And mine just happened to be of the huge variety."

"That's in the past now." He gently brushed a strand of hair out of her face and tucked it behind her ear. "Weren't you the one who talked to me about change and redemption and all of that?"

She smiled. "Yes. It's just that…over the last few days I've had to relive all of this, and it really pulls me back to a dark place I don't want to go. Then I start thinking about who I was then and how lost I was. I never want to feel that way again."

He cupped her cheek with his hand. "You don't have to. I'm right here, and I'm not going anywhere."

"I know I've said it before, but thank you, Max. For everything. Not just for putting your life on the line for me, but for your friendship through this awful time."

"I'd do it again in a heartbeat. And I should be the one thanking you for leading me back to my faith. I didn't even realize how tired and drained I was from being so hard-hearted. I've been doing a lot of thinking about and it, and I realize now that I shouldn't have ever linked my parents and their problems to God. To know that I'm moving past that is huge for me. And I never would've started down that path without your example."

She took his hand in hers. "It's God who was at work in both of our lives."

* * *

Max anxiously awaited Tom's return. Tom had called to say he would be back at the house soon and would be bringing a couple of agents with him. Maybe Tom had decided not to slow down the plan they'd discussed just because Davies had been killed.

Tom came barreling through the front door with two men by his side. After introducing FBI agents Clive Roberts and Shay Hall, Tom took a seat at the head of the dining-room table. Sydney, who had insisting on being involved in the initial meeting, sat across from him with her hands folded on the table and her eyes on Tom.

"First, let me update you on what we know so far about Davies," Tom said. "He died of a single gunshot wound to the head. Looks like a professional hit. We're working the scene and will have more information about ballistics soon. At this point, we're working with the theory that things between Davies and East River started going south. That's the best motive we have right now, and when you think about it for a minute it seems the most plausible."

Max nodded. "Any time you have a situation like that, it's bound to go sour. It's only a matter of when not if. And Davies served his purpose. East River has plenty of other thugs who can do their dirty work. Once Davies's cover was blown with the Marshals, he really lost his usefulness."

"So what do we do now?" Sydney asked.

"I think it's time to move forward with the plan we discussed," Tom said. "Clive and Shay will have you under surveillance from this time forward. I know we'd talked about having you go home, but I don't think that makes a lot of sense. Max would still assume you were in some danger, and he'd want to keep you on the move. So after I thought about it, it seems the better play is to have you keep moving around. Hopefully, this won't take that long. You two will need to get out and about but not be overly conspicuous about it."

Sydney leaned forward. "What about the tracking device?"

"That's totally up to you. I have an FBI tracker here with me. Basically it's given to you like an injection. It inserts the chip right under your skin. The removal would require you to be cut open just a little and then stitched. I think it's overkill, but I brought it. I'll do whatever you're comfortable with."

"I want to do it, but can I just have a minute?" Sydney asked.

"Sure, we can go over some of the logistics."

"I'll be back in a few." Sydney stood up from the table and walked out of the room.

Max thought for a moment about going after her, but he wanted to give her some time alone. If it were purely up to him, she'd definitely have the tracker for his own peace of mind.

"All right," Max said. "We'll leave here in a bit and go grab some food in public. Then we'll drive around for a little while and head to the first hotel. I'll text you guys the hotel address before we leave the restaurant."

For a few minutes they reviewed the plan, until Sydney walked back into the room.

"Let's move forward with the tracking device. I'm not worried about having it removed afterward. I'm hoping that it will be overkill just like you said. But the last thing I want is for something to go wrong and be alone with Rick with no way of anyone knowing where I am."

"We won't let that happen," Tom said. "But I think you're making the right decision. If nothing else, it will give you peace of mind."

"Then I'm ready," Sydney said.

But was Max?

The next two days passed by slowly as Sydney and Max struggled to get into a routine that wasn't exactly routine.

Sydney knocked on the adjoining hotel room

door, ready to go on her next outing—this time to the park for a jog.

He opened the door and gave her a smile.

"How long do you think we're going to have to go on these fake trips until Rick decides to act?" she asked.

"I told you before that I didn't think it would happen immediately."

She nodded. "I know I need to be more patient, but it's difficult."

"You ready for our jog?"

"Yes."

He grabbed her hand. "And you remember the plan? I'm going to fake pain in my arm from getting shot the other day. I'll stop and take a breather, and you'll keep running. Our surveillance team will be in place, and I'll be there. So there's no need for you to be concerned."

She laughed. "Weren't you the one just the other day talking about how dangerous this was?"

"Well, I feel better now that we have a concrete system. The FBI guys are on top of things. I'm impressed with Clive and Shay."

"I hope you have fun feigning shoulder pain while I'm the one doing all the work."

"Hey now, don't give me grief." He smiled.

"Although at some point it will feel pretty good to get back into my gym routine."

Suddenly she felt the seriousness of the situation. She couldn't pretend to find any humor in it. Her smile faded, replaced by sadness and regret.

She lowered her gaze, "Since I came into your life you're not doing anything that you would normally do."

With his index finger he raised her chin so that she could see the look on his face. "But since you came into my life, it's gotten a lot better. In pretty much every way."

"You're sweet to say that."

"I'm saying it because it's true. I know you're hesitant about moving into any relationship. Based on everything you've gone through, it's totally understandable. And before I met you I thought there was almost zero chance that I'd ever find anyone that I really wanted to have in my life." He put his hands on her shoulders. "But what we have going on here between us, Syd, is real. I feel it in my gut. I feel it like I've never felt anything before. I'm pulled toward you. And not just because you're so talented and witty and beautiful. It's much more than that. You're so much more than that."

She was so moved by his words that she couldn't form any of her own. She looked up into his eyes. It wasn't as if he hadn't made his feelings known before, but in that moment, she was swamped with emotion, feeling both excited and fearful. She honestly didn't know if she could ever let a man back into her life in a romantic way. She was certain that the Lord had sent Max into her life. But that didn't mean they were supposed to be a couple. If all she had was his friendship, then she could probably live with that.

While she hesitated to reply, Max went into marshal mode. "While I'd much rather stay here with you and act like nothing was going on in the world out there, we both know that isn't the case. So we should probably go now," he said.

He was right. Unless they put their plan into action, this nightmare would never end.

To the world they looked like just an average couple dressed in T-shirts and sweatpants ready to take a jog in the park. But they were anything but average at this point.

That very thought sent a chill down her arms.

He noticed her shiver. "You can't be cold?"

"No. It's just a little case of the nerves. I'll be fine, though." She walked out of the hotel room with him right by her side.

By the time they got to the park, she was actually ready to run. "Getting out and breathing the fresh air is actually just what I need," she said.

They walked up the running trail and stretched for a minute. Then she touched his arm. "I'm ready. Let's go."

He laughed. "All right then, boss. You lead the way. Set the pace."

"Sounds good to me." She looked around and saw a few other people in the park with children and dogs. A couple of other people were running. But it definitely wasn't crowded since it was a weekday. This was the second day in a row they'd gone running. The hope was that Rick or his people from East River would notice a pattern. Her concern was what if she was wrong? What if he didn't come after her now? The thought of waiting for some undetermined time for him to strike made her crazy.

She started jogging down the trail, and Max was right beside her step for step. The only sounds were the pounding of their feet against the ground. They kept a steady pace that was comfortable for her. The wind blew lightly and the sun was out and shining brightly down on them.

For a moment she allowed herself to think that this was like any other day. And that she was on a nice jog with her friend. Max may want more, but did he understand what it would be like to be in a true relationship?

She decided to say something. "Max, I know everything about what we're doing here has been a bit unconventional, to say the least. Do you really think that once this is all over that you'd be able to handle a normal relationship?"

"I surely hope so." He laughed. "Where did that come from?"

"I was just thinking about everything we've been through. I think your feelings for me might be impacted by the danger we're in and your natural inclination to serve as a protector. Once that's over, you may go back to your regular self. The guy who doesn't show emotion and has the walls built up. The guy who doesn't really want to be in a relationship with anyone."

"I don't think that's going to happen, Syd. I've really thought about everything. The road back to faith has forced me to grapple with a lot of things that only I can deal with on my own—and with God. But we both know that I'm not the man you first met. So much has changed in my heart and mind. I can't deny your involvement in this process. And, no, I'm not perfect. I'm sure I'm going to struggle with showing my emotions for the rest of my life.

It's not like a light switch I can easily flip on and off. But I want to try because I don't like the shell of a man that I had become."

He sounded so convincing. She wondered if they really could have a chance. But right now she didn't know. "I'm glad that you feel like you're making positive changes" was all she said. All she could say. She steadied her breathing and settled into the jog.

After a few minutes Max pulled up short. "My shoulder."

She stopped beside him. "You're hurting. You need to rest for a minute. I'll wait with you." They were going through the motions just as they'd discussed.

He bent over. "Yeah, the running is starting to bother my whole arm and shoulder."

She leaned down toward him. "What can I do?"

"Don't let me hold you up. You keep on going."

He'd insisted that they act this out with dialogue even though it was unlikely anyone would be close enough to hear exactly what they were saying even if they were being followed.

"All right. If you're sure. I'll just finish my loop and meet you here on my way back, unless you're able to walk to the starting point before then."

"I'll be fine. Don't worry about me. Go ahead."

She took off running down the trail by herself. Or at least it felt as though she was completely alone even though she knew that the two FBI agents were somewhere close by. Max had insisted he knew where they were, but Sydney had never been able to notice their presence.

She took in a deep breath and allowed herself to enjoy the movement. After feeling so confined lately, this bit of freedom was a welcome respite.

When she heard the sound of footsteps approach from behind, she turned to look but saw it was just another jogger. He smiled at her and breezed right on by.

Am I running that slowly? Just like Max, she'd been out of practice with her normal exercise routine and her intense self-defense training, which was an amazing workout and another reason she was eager to get back to her regular life. But her life would never really be regular again. Not as long as Max was in it. How would they work things out once this was all resolved?

Would Max want to keep working as a marshal? She'd support him in whatever decision he made, although it made her nervous to think of him staying in such a dangerous profession. But she'd never hold him back from what he was so good at.

If someone tried to stop her from doing her work, she wouldn't be very happy with that. He actually seemed to have a bit more understanding of the work she did as a forensic artist now. All she asked was that he didn't put her down like Rick had. After Max had seen her testimony, he'd acted as if he respected her work a lot more. That meant so much to her. She wanted him to believe in her.

While she didn't feel too great about her security situation and revisiting her past, she felt a flood of optimism about the possibility of at least a continued friendship with Max. She'd reserve judgment on anything more for now. *Lord, can I ever trust another man enough to be in a romantic relationship again?*

"Ugh." Her shoelace on her right foot had become untied and was going to cause her problems if she didn't stop and retie it. She was enjoying her run so much she hated to break her rhythm. But she leaned over to reach toward her shoe and as she did, a gunshot rang out. Instinctually, she hit the ground and started to bear crawl to the shrubbery on the side of the trail.

She heard another shot, but then male voices rang out loudly. That had to be her FBI escort. Crouching down low behind the shrubs she waited. She wasn't going to take any chances.

And then it occurred to her that if she wouldn't have stopped and leaned over to tie her shoe she might be dead right now. *Thank You, Lord, for watching out for me, yet again.*

Looking down she saw her hands were shaking, but she was alive.

"Sydney!"

She instantly recognized Max's voice.

"Over here," she yelled.

He came running to where she was hiding. "Are you okay?"

"Yes, but it was close, Max. If I wouldn't have bent down to tie my shoe…" She paused and looked up at him. "I think I would've been hit."

"I don't know what all happened. When I heard the shots I came running, but it looked like the FBI agents have the shooter in custody."

"Anyone you recognize?"

"No. I've never seen him before." He took her hand and pulled her up from the ground and into a big hug. "I am so glad you're all right. When I heard that shot, all I could think of was how this plan had gone wrong."

"I'm not going to lie. That was close."

"We need to rethink our strategy. This plan was all premised on the idea that Rick would want to take you alive, and more specifically, that he would be the guy to come after you. Once the shooter doesn't go back, the East River guys will know something happened."

She nodded. "This definitely didn't go as I wanted it to. Rick is nowhere to be found, and he sent some other random East River guy to take me out."

"We don't know that for sure, but that's a totally reasonable assumption. Let's get you out of here."

"We're going to have to adjust the strategy," Tom said. It was a couple of hours later, and they'd regrouped at their current safe house.

"What is the guy who was apprehended saying?"

"He lawyered up immediately. Didn't say a word, and frankly, I'm not expecting him to. He's much more afraid of East River than he is of law enforcement."

Elena walked into the kitchen. Max wasn't expecting to see her. "Hey, everyone. I bring news from the US Marshals."

"What kind of news?" Max asked.

Elena sighed. "Not the kind you're going to

want." She took a seat at the table joining him, Tom and Sydney.

"I made another pitch to the Marshals based on the current set of facts. But they think this is purely FBI territory right now. They're not denying that Sydney is in danger, but no one who has any power at the Marshals thinks this has anything to do with Sydney's testimony against Kevin Diaz. And Diaz was acquitted and is back to leading his regular life. A pillar of the community and all of that. Honestly, I think there may be some at the Marshals who are afraid to overreach on this for repercussions to their careers. Diaz is connected to a lot of powerful people."

"Thanks for trying to get me additional help," Sydney said.

"I'm sorry I wasn't more successful, but this is the end of the line. And it also looks like my time at the Marshals is drawing to a close. There's going to be a review board hearing next month about how I handled the Davies situation. Until then I'm on administrative leave. Even though I ended up being right about his involvement with East River, I didn't follow protocol. In fact, I broke almost every rule in the book. I'm already prepared to move on, but I just wanted to let you know about that."

"Oh, Elena. Is there anything I could do to

vouch for you?" Sydney asked. "You did what you thought was best at the time."

Elena shook her head. "No, Sydney. In retrospect, it was definitely the wrong move. I've had plenty of time to go over it again and again in my head. I should've never kept the information from Max. Since he was in charge of your security, my actions could have caused you grave harm." She paused. "But enough about me. I just wanted everyone to know what was going on. Given everything that's happened, I should probably not be involved in any of your active FBI operations. I don't want to get in more trouble than I already am. But if you get in a bind and need me, all you need to do is ask."

"Thanks, Elena," Max said. "I'm sure I'll be exiting the Marshals right behind you. Even though I've taken a leave of absence, they aren't going to like what I've been doing." He ran his hand through his hair. "But I guess I'll cross that bridge when I get to it. My number one priority right now is Sydney."

"I'm going to go. I'll let you all get back to it. Call me if you need me." Elena stood, walked to Sydney and gave her shoulder a squeeze. Max hated seeing Elena's career destroyed over this, but she had made a mistake. He could forgive her, but a strike like that against her record would stifle forever any career advancement possibilities at the Marshals.

After Elena had left, Tom stood and leaned against his chair. "I'm calling off the current operation. We made some assumptions that appeared to be flawed. Including the fact that Rick was so obsessed with Sydney that he would personally be the one to come after her." Tom took a step away from the chair and crossed his arms. "What that tells me is that Rick is worried about getting caught. Yes, he wants his revenge against Sydney, but he also doesn't want to go back to jail."

"Yeah, we made the wrong assumption," Max said.

"With the current set of facts I'm not willing to keep putting Sydney out there in harm's way, purposely trying to draw Ward out." Tom turned to her. "I think you need to lie low until we come up with a better plan."

"You're not going to give up on finding Rick, are you?" Sydney asked with wide eyes.

"No. I'm definitely not giving up. Just reassessing what's the best way to get to him. And I have to be honest with you, Sydney. This may be a long-term issue. You may want to consider leaving the state and going somewhere far away."

"But I don't want to hide," she said loudly.

"I have a career. I want to get back to my job, to my life." She looked down and then back up at Tom. "Rick Ward has already taken so much from me. I refuse to go into hiding and let him keep taking from me."

"Just think about it," Tom said. "And in the meantime, the plan will be for you two to stay locked down."

Max could tell by looking at Sydney that she wasn't going to go on the run. He just hoped that she wouldn't attempt to do anything drastic.

THIRTEEN

"I can't keep living like this," Sydney said. It'd been two weeks on almost complete lockdown, and she had about had it.

"I'm sorry, Syd. But Tom will be here soon to take you to consult on that case you were contacted about. At least that will get your mind off of things."

"What are you going to do while I'm gone?" she asked Max.

"Hit the gym and the grocery store. Just moving forward and trying to keep it all in perspective."

"I know. And I'm sorry you have to hear me complain. It's not you that I'm upset at or even Tom. It's Rick and the entire East River operation." She took a breath. "And seeing Kevin Diaz on the nightly news is making me lose my mind. When he did that interview about being falsely accused, I could barely keep it together."

"One thing I've learned from all my years

in law enforcement is that people like him are never one-time offenders."

"But don't you see? That's the problem. Some other innocent woman will probably be killed because of me failing in my testimony against him."

"Don't think about that right now, Syd. Focus on your witness consultation."

"Thanks, Max. I feel like every job I have from here on out will always be about redeeming myself."

"One case at a time, Syd."

Tom came through the door. "Sorry I'm running a few minutes late. You ready to go, Sydney?"

"Definitely." She grabbed the bag that held her laptop and supplies. Looking over at Max, she smiled. "I'll be back in a few hours. Have a good workout."

"See you soon."

Sydney followed Tom out to his dark sedan. "Thanks for setting this up and for taking me. Going back to work is exactly what I need right now."

He opened the car door for her and she got in. He joined her a minute later and started up the engine.

"I'm just glad I could work this out. I know you'll get a little boost from this meeting.

According to the local police, the witness is very anxious and scared. I think you'll be just what she needs to calm down."

"Working one on one with the witnesses is probably my most favorite part about the job."

Sydney's cell phone rang and she saw it was Max calling. "That's Max. Wonder what he could want since we just left."

She pressed talk. "Hey, what's going on?"

"Brian's asking for me at the hospital."

"Why? Is he okay?"

"I'm not sure. But I'm going over there now. I just wanted to let you know."

"Sure. Be careful." She ended the call.

"What did he want?" Tom asked as he tapped his fingers on the steering wheel.

"He's going to visit Brian."

"Really?"

"Yeah, he just wanted to let me know where he'd be."

Tom nodded. "Shouldn't be long and we'll be at the station."

Max entered Brian's room after getting cleared by the police officer stationed outside the door. No one was convinced Brian wasn't still a target of East River.

"Brian, are you okay?" He pulled up a chair beside the bed.

"My memory," Brian said. "It's starting to come back to me."

He smiled. Finally some good news. "That's great."

"You would think so, but I'm having some really bad and confusing memories."

"That's to be expected. You took a real beating while you were being held by East River."

"It's not that part that I'm so concerned about." He looked away and then made direct eye contact. "I'm about to tell you something, but you have to keep this to yourself in case I'm totally wrong or delusional. The doctor did say that it was perfectly normal for my memories to be jumbled. But I felt like I just had to say something because what I'm remembering just won't go away. If anything, these specific thoughts just become more persistent by the minute."

Max wondered if Brian was having some type of PTSD. "Whatever it is, Brian, I'm here for you. And if you need to talk to a professional, I'm sure we'll get you the best one the FBI has."

Brian shook his head. "It's not like that, Max." He paused. "How do I even say this?"

"Take your time."

Brian nodded. "I keep having these flashbacks. I was locked in a room and different

East River guys were in and out, including Rick Ward. Davies was the one who initially kidnapped me—that I know for sure—but I didn't really see much of him after that. This was mainly an internal East River operation."

"Okay, then what happened?"

"They beat me up pretty bad on multiple occasions. But here's the thing." Brian took a deep breath, and Max could tell this was difficult for him.

"Whatever it is, we can handle it together."

"I heard a voice a couple of times in that room. Talking about strategy and tactics. They probably thought I was passed out from the pain because I usually kept my eyes closed to conserve what little energy I had."

"What about the voice is bothering you?"

"It's a voice I'd recognize anywhere, Max."

"Who?"

"It was Tom Hilton. The voice I heard was Tom's."

Max gasped as though he'd been punched in the gut. "Are you sure?"

"I know you probably doubt my sanity right now. And is it possible that I'm totally off base and delusional? I guess so. But I know my own thoughts, and I definitely know the man I've worked with for years. It was him, Max. Tom was in that room."

As Brian's words hit him, Max felt as though the room was closing in on him.

"Max, say something. Are you all right?"

Max shook his head and stood up. "No. No. This can't be happening." He paced around the small hospital room for a minute to gather his thoughts. But he knew exactly what he had to do.

"I'm sorry, Max. I just had to talk about it."

"He has Sydney," Max whispered.

"Who has Sydney?"

"Tom. He picked her up to take her to a witness consultation. This is her first attempt at going back to work. He offered to take her, in fact." Max looked at Brian. "I've got to go. I have to make sure she's okay."

"For her sake, I hope I'm wrong, Max. Please know that."

Max was already running out of the hospital room—and saying a prayer.

He pulled out his cell and called her. It went straight to voicemail. Oh, no, he thought. What if he was too late?

Then he remembered her tracking chip. The only problem was that he needed an FBI agent to be able to access the chip. And at this point he had no idea if the two agents Tom had brought in were trustworthy or if only Tom was dirty.

He told himself to take a deep breath and think. It was entirely possible that Brian was delusional. He'd gone through a terribly traumatic event. But Max wasn't going to bank on that.

What he needed to do was call the local police and see if Sydney had made it to the meeting.

Fifteen minutes later after jumping through hoops, he got the answer he feared the most. Sydney had never arrived at the station.

Sydney looked forward to this meeting. Getting back out there and focusing on her work—what she loved—was really what she needed. Lately her world had been consumed with threats and looking back to the past.

Tom's phone rang and he answered it. She could only hear his side of the conversation, but she could immediately tell she wasn't going to like what was happening.

"There's been a security breach at the police station," he explained once he disconnected the call. "It's not safe for you there now."

"Are you taking me back to the safe house?"

"No. It's best if I take you to a new place. I have another safe house we can go to."

"All right. Let me call Max and let him know so he won't worry."

She pulled out her phone.

"I can't let you do that."

She looked up and her stomach clenched. *No. This can't be.*

But it was. Tom's left hand was on the wheel but his right hand was holding a gun, and it was pointed right at her.

"Just put down the phone, Sydney. I don't want to have to use this."

She slowly set the phone on her lap. "Why, Tom? Why would you do this?"

"Now's not the time for you to be asking questions. Just stay quiet and we'll be there in a bit."

Was he going to turn her over to Rick? *Dear Lord, please help me now.*

Tom drove outside the city to a more rural area. He pulled down a dirt road and drove up to a red farmhouse. The area surrounding the house was heavily wooded.

Still holding his gun, Tom opened his car door and walked around to the passenger side.

"Get out slowly."

"Please, Tom. Don't do this. Don't throw away your entire career over me."

He grabbed her arm, pulled her out of the car. "I tried to give you the chance to get out of this by suggesting that you leave the state and disappear. But you didn't take that advice. This is much bigger than you, Sydney." He dragged her up to the front door and into the farmhouse. "And don't even think about that tracking device helping you. Remember, I'm the one that injected you, so I have control over the tracking technology, and I've already deactivated it manually."

Her heart sank at that revelation. She needed to buy time. And she prayed that Rick wasn't somewhere in that house.

"Tom, I've gotten to know you. Would you really turn me over to that monster knowing what he's done to me?"

Tom looked down. "Ward is now the number two in East River, and that's why you're here. What Ward wants, he gets. I'm in no position to question him. I have my own problems to contend with."

"But you could've turned me over to him before. Why now?"

He let out a loud sigh. "Because I needed to keep my position at the FBI for as long as possible. Taking you would've added complications that we didn't need." He brought out his handcuffs and pulled her into the bathroom where he secured her to the pipe under the sink. "You're going to hang out here while I handle a few things."

"Were the other agents you brought in to help me in on this, too?"

He shook his head. "No. My circle is tighter than that." He walked out of the bathroom leaving her alone.

A million thoughts flooded her mind. She tugged against the pipe to see how sturdy it was. Unfortunately, it didn't budge. She had to find a way out of there before Rick showed up. She'd hoped that she could get through to Tom, but she was starting to think that for Tom this wasn't about her. What had he gotten himself into? He must be knee deep in with East River.

Would Max be able to find her in time? She could only pray he would. And that she'd somehow get out of this alive.

Max called Elena. They both agreed it was worth the risk to reach out to the two FBI agents who had been working with Tom. They had no other choice. They needed to know if the agents were in Tom's pocket. Clive Roberts and Shay Hall met him at the safe house.

"We have an issue," Max said.

"What is it?" Clive asked.

Max proceeded to tell them what Brian had told him and that Sydney and Tom were currently MIA. As he explained, he and Elena watched them carefully to read their expressions and body language. Confident they were not in league with the rogue agent, he nodded at Elena who returned the gesture.

"You think Tom is working with East River?" Clive asked.

"Yes. And now he's taken Sydney."

"That's just unbelievable," Shay said.

Elena took a step closer to the agents. "Right now we need your help. You have access to the tracking chip."

"Oh, yeah, right." Clive pulled out his phone and a moment later blew out a breath. "I'm sorry. It looks like it was deactivated on the FBI side."

"Tom's responsible for that," Max said. "Can you reactivate it?"

"I can't but Shay's the tech guy."

Shay looked at Max. "I'm not supposed to do it because it will require me to break some technical security protocols."

Max stepped closer. "An innocent woman's life is on the line."

"Understood," Shay said. "Let me get my laptop out of the car and start working on it."

"Assuming we get a location, what next?" Clive asked.

"We get out to her as fast as we can, and we have to be ready to be met with resistance. I'm not sure what Tom is up to here, but whatever it is, it isn't good."

"He's been running the East River task force for years," Clive said, shaking his head.

Max nodded. "I know. I can't believe they got to him."

"I'm going to get on the phone with my bosses at the Marshals," Elena said. "Maybe once they hear all of this, they'll provide some assistance."

Max walked outside for a minute to clear his head. *Dear Lord, I'm scared to death that something is going to happen to Sydney and that I won't be there to protect her. God, I don't know what I will do without her in my life. Please help her and help me. Give me the strength to know what I need to do.*

Max found a brief moment of solace in his prayer. But he couldn't just sit around and wait. He walked back inside where Shay was banging away on the keys of his laptop at the kitchen table.

"I don't have to tell you that every minute counts," Max said.

"Roger that."

Elena walked into the kitchen. "It's a no go from the Marshals. They don't want to touch this. It's a no win for them. I'm sorry, Max. We're on our own here."

"Got it," Shay yelled.

Max pushed away the bad news from Elena and stood over Shay's shoulder.

"Assuming the device is still implanted, I've got the address."

"We could really use your help. Are you two guys in on this?" Max asked.

"Yes," Clive and Shay said in unison.

Shay looked back down at the laptop. "Forty-five minutes to get there."

"Let's move." Max walked out of the kitchen and went on the most important mission of his life.

Sydney heard the front door open and close multiple times. Then Tom walked into the bathroom.

"Time to get up," he barked at her.

"Where are we going?"

Tom didn't say anything as he unlocked her handcuffs. She rubbed her left wrist.

As he guided her into the living room, she came face to face with her worst nightmare.

"If it isn't my favorite ex-girlfriend."

Rick stood there smiling. But it wasn't a friendly one. Every nerve in her body tingled, and her chest tightened so badly she could barely take in a shallow breath.

"Tom, you can leave us now. I'm good." Even the sound of his voice sent chills up her spine.

"Are you sure?" Tom asked.

She pleaded with Tom using her eyes, but he looked away.

"Yeah, get out of here. You did your part. Lucas wants to talk to you about the next steps. So you should call him ASAP." Rick turned his attention back to her.

Despite how she felt, she forced herself to stand up straight and look him in the eyes. She refused to show him her fear.

"You've become a thorn in my side for a while now, Sydney. Before I thought you were harmless, but little did I know that you were going to become the state's star witness against Kevin Diaz."

"That trial is over," she replied. "He was acquitted."

Rick took a step closer to her, but she held her ground.

"Yeah, because you choked. Guess I was right about your little hobby after all."

That was a direct verbal hit. He knew how to belittle her. But she merely let it fuel her resolve. She raised her chin and met his eyes squarely. "What's your play here, Rick? Why even bother with me? Don't you have much more pressing East River business to deal with?"

"You've embarrassed me, Sydney. I can't let that go unpunished."

"What do you want from me?"

"You. Plain and simple. Come back to me. Play the part I will need you to play. You'd have to quit working for the cops, but I'd provide whatever you needed. I'm in a much different financial position than I was years ago."

Was he crazy? Maybe. "Are you asking me to be your girlfriend?" Her voice went up an octave in surprise.

"I know you've got something going on with that marshal. Leave him and come back to me. I'll spare your life."

Yeah, right. Until he got mad and beat her again. No way. But the longer she could keep him talking the more chances she would give herself to escape. "I don't understand why you'd want me again."

"I see a different person now than you used to be. You grew a backbone. At first I had planned to seek my revenge and move on. But now I find myself thinking about different options." He took a breath. "But make no mistake, if I can't have you, then nobody will."

"Is that why you sent someone to shoot me at the park and at the safe house?"

"The orders were to kill the marshal. Not you."

She couldn't help but laugh. "Your men need to learn the difference between a man and a woman, then. Because on the trail, I was jogging alone when the shot went off."

"That was Tom's doing. He acted without thinking. He never should have allowed that guy to take the shot."

"How is he involved in all of this, anyway?"

Rick blew out a breath. "Tom has been up to his eyeballs in this for years, Sydney."

"Years?"

"Yes. I've known him since I first joined East River."

"And now you're working directly with the leader, Lucas Jones?"

He walked over to her and ran his hand down her cheek. "Aren't you inquisitive?"

She tried not to shake when he touched her. He'd always been like this. One minute gentle and seemingly rational. The next minute on a rampage. "If you want me to come back to you, I'm just trying to figure out where everything stands."

He nodded. "Yes, I've been working with

Lucas very closely. I took the fall for his little brother in that robbery charge, and he owes me. So he brought me into the leadership. I'm making more money than I've ever seen in my life."

"And Kevin Diaz is involved with Lucas and East River, right?"

His eyes widened for a second as his face reddened in anger. "Wouldn't you like to know?" He took a step toward her. Then his cell phone rang, and he walked over to the kitchen counter to pick it up.

It only took her a millisecond to make the decision. She bolted for the front door. And ran.

FOURTEEN

Sydney ran as fast as she could out the front door, down the steps and toward the woods that surrounded the farmhouse. She had to run for the woods because she'd be a sitting duck on the open dirt road.

"Sydney!" Rick's angry voice roared behind her.

But the good news was it didn't sound as though he was that close to her. And she definitely wasn't taking the chance to turn around and look. No, she pressed forward, running faster than she ever had. She prayed that with each step she was putting more distance between her and the man who almost destroyed her life multiple times.

The woods got more dense the farther she ran. Branches scraped her face and arms, but she didn't slow down. Couldn't. Wouldn't.

Soon the brush got so thick it took a lot of strength just to push the heavy branches back and make her way through it. Finally, she stole a glance behind her. She couldn't see anyone. Just the thick woods. It was much darker now because of the tree cover.

Taking a moment to catch her breath, she looked around to try to get a lay of the land. But everything looked the same. She needed to find something that was large enough to provide her with some cover.

Right now trees were her best option, but maybe if she ventured farther there would be some shelter where she could hide.

She could try to outrun him, but eventually he would catch up. She'd be better off to fortify herself and wait, then catch him off guard and fight him. Or, even better, maybe help would come soon. She could only pray for that.

Max had never driven so fast in his life.

"Two minutes out," Elena said from the passenger seat. "We're about to hit all dirt roads."

"This is the middle of nowhere," Max said, checking his rearview where he saw Clive and Shay following right behind him. He held the wheel tightly, trying to keep his nerves in check. All that mattered to him was rescuing Sydney. He wasn't able to fathom moving on in life without her. She was his rock. "I still can't believe Tom would do this."

"Maybe they're blackmailing him. Or maybe he got tired of a government salary and decided to go to the dark side."

"Tom was one of the people who suggested I'd be a great marshal. Looking back on it, he was probably trying to get rid of me."

"That's totally possible." She paused. "This turn on your left is it."

He swung the car down the street which was another dirt road. Nothing was in sight except trees on each side and then a big pasture up ahead.

"Keep driving. About a mile more."

"I'll stop about a quarter mile out so we can make our approach on foot. Who knows what we're about to walk into."

"We should be prepared for just about anything," she said.

But he wasn't prepared for another car to come barreling down the street right at them.

"That's Tom's car," Max said. "Hold on." Max jerked the wheel, putting his car directly in the path of Tom's. He braced for impact and told Elena to do the same. His side of the car would take the brunt of the hit if Tom didn't stop.

The sound of squealing breaks filled the air, until finally Tom's car came to a stop just inches from his own. Pulling his gun, he jumped out of the car and approached Tom's car from the driver's side, as Elena did the same from the passenger side. Tom slowly opened the door with his gun in hand.

"Drop the gun, Tom. It's over."

It was two against one and Tom knew it. Yeah, he could get off one shot, but then he'd be killed the next moment. Unless Tom wanted to die, he would drop his weapon.

Slowly, as he exited the car, he placed his gun on the ground.

"Where's Sydney?" Max asked.

"She's at a farmhouse down the way."

"Is Ward with her?"

"Yes."

"Elena, deal with him, I'm going to the farmhouse." He heard the sound of the other car behind him. But he wasn't going to waste another second. Not when Sydney was alone with that man. "Tell Clive and Shay to come after me."

He jumped in the car and floored it, dirt flying everywhere. *Please, dear Lord, don't let him have hurt her.* That's all he could think about until the farmhouse was in sight.

Then he slammed on the brakes, checked his gun and started running toward the house. Yes, it would've been more pragmatic to wait for backup, but every second counted right now.

Besides, he knew the two agents were literally right behind him.

He bounded up the steps and opened the door, which was unlocked.

"Sydney!" he yelled.

No one replied as he went room to room clearing the house. As soon as he finished each room check, he walked back into the living room and saw Clive and Shay coming in.

"No one's here," Max said.

"Maybe she made a run for it," Clive said.

"Those woods are really thick." Shay pulled out his phone and showed the two of them the aerial view. "Her tracking chip isn't providing a strong enough signal to provide an exact location."

"We have to look for her," Max said. "Because if she did get away, I'm sure that Ward is out there trying to track her down, too."

Clive nodded. "This is a dead-end road. Only one way out. And there's still a black truck parked out front."

"I assume that's Ward's truck," Max replied.

"Okay, then, let's split up and search the woods," Shay said.

"Do we get cell service way out here?" Max asked.

"Yes, a weak signal," Shay said. "But I can't

say what will happen when we get deep in the woods with all the tree cover."

They divided up the search quadrant the best they could with the technology they had. Max didn't want to wait another second. He jogged off into the woods.

He had to find her. He wouldn't even consider the alternative. The good news was that it looked as though she had gotten away from Ward. But the bad news was that Ward had a head start on him and would likely be really angry about Sydney's evasion.

As he got farther into the woods, the foliage got thicker. As he pushed through the branches, he winced at the pain from his gunshot wound but kept moving. The thought of Sydney having to go through that alone only powered him forward. That and his renewed faith. A faith that she helped guide him toward.

With each step he took deeper into the woods, his determination grew. With all of his heart and soul he wanted a life with Sydney. He only regretted that he hadn't fully told her how he felt. With every fiber of his being, he hoped to have that opportunity. Because if he did get it, he promised himself he wouldn't mess it up.

Sydney had finally calmed down and willed herself to take slow deep breaths. Hiding low on the ground behind two big trees, she felt somewhat fortified. Obviously, she lacked a gun, which would've been the best defense. But at least if she stayed here, she'd be able to hear anyone approaching and would have the element of surprise on her side.

She wondered if Max had figured out yet what was happening. She didn't want to die like this. It wasn't because she was afraid of dying. It was that she was afraid of missing the chance to have a life with Max. A life she'd thought she could never have until now. Yeah, they had their differences, but they'd grown so much together. She'd come to realize how strong she had become.

To see him transform in front of her had been amazing. God's fingerprints were all over their relationship. And she was so thankful for that. She was willing to fight for him, and to fight to protect herself.

The woman she'd been when she'd met Rick Ward was completely foreign to her. At least she'd moved past the shame and embarrassment of it all.

The sound of a stick crunching broke her out of her thoughts. She went on high alert. Careful not to make a move, she cast a watchful eye at her surroundings.

Then she heard the unmistakable sound of

footsteps getting closer to her location. This was it.

Rick stalked toward her. He hadn't noticed her yet, and she used that to her advantage. Just as he was walking by her, she stuck out her leg—tripping him and causing him to hit the ground with a thud.

Before he could react, she kicked him hard in the ribs and then delivered a second kick to the temple.

But Rick was over six feet and two hundred pounds. Her efforts, while strong, didn't completely take him out.

He yelled foul names at her as he attempted to stand. Before he could get fully to his feet, she delivered yet another kick to the same area of the ribs. Then she thrust the palm of her hand hard up against his nose—and heard a loud crunch of bones. She'd certainly broken his nose.

Blood started to pour down his face. Like a wild animal he charged her. She quickly sidestepped his approach.

But then he circled her and came from behind putting his hands were on her. His grip was so tight she thought he may break her in two.

"You are so stupid," he spat out. "I gave you a way out. The perfect life. And you rejected me again." After adding another set of insults, he turned her around to face him.

He wrapped his big hands around her neck and squeezed. "I want you to have to look in my eyes as I kill you."

His grip was so tight she had no doubt of his intentions. She started to pray, knowing that this could be the end. She tried to stomp her foot on his, but his hands were so strong around her neck she could barely move.

"Drop your hands now or I'll shoot you." The deep voice rang out in the woods.

Was it Max? Or was she delirious from the loss of blood flow to her brain? When he repeated his command, she knew it was really him. He'd come for her.

But now she feared Rick would kill them both. She knew Rick had a gun, even though the weapon he was using on her right now was his bare hands.

"You don't have the shot," Rick said with confidence. "You wouldn't take the risk of shooting your worthless girlfriend."

"Don't try me."

"Then go ahead and take the shot."

Sydney braced herself for the gun blast, but it never came.

After a second, Rick laughed. "I knew you didn't have the skill or the backbone to attempt a move like that. So here's how this is going to go down. Sydney is eventually going to die. That is not negotiable. Your only chance of getting out of these woods tonight and having any semblance of a life is if you drop your gun and kick it over to me. Then I'll consider letting you live, but Sydney comes with me. This is your chance to save yourself. Don't give up your life over a woman."

His grip was still strong around her neck but not as tight as before. She was able to pull in some air and turn slightly to make eye contact with Max. They'd done this before with Davies—communicated without words. Her eyes told him he could make the shot. She just needed to give him a tiny bit of room to work with.

"I'm counting to five and if you don't drop the gun, she'll die right here and now with you watching." Rick squeezed his hands tighter around her neck. "It's your move, marshal."

Rick started to count. When he got to five, she used all her strength to drop down low just as the shot rang out. Blood splattered her but Rick's grip completely released from her neck.

Max ran over as Rick fell to the ground. "Are you all right?" he asked her.

"Uh, I think so." She started to shake as she looked down and saw Rick covered with blood from a gunshot wound to the head.

"I didn't want to kill him, but I had to aim high to make sure I wouldn't hit you. I'm sorry, Syd." He bent down and checked for a pulse. He shook his head. "He's gone."

"You just saved my life." Her voice was hoarse from being choked. She touched her hand to her neck and it was tender.

"He hurt you. I'm so sorry I couldn't get here faster." He wrapped his arms around her waist.

"Is it really over?"

"Yes, it is, Syd. You're safe now. Rick can never hurt you again."

Male voices rang out and were moving closer.

"Over here," he yelled. "That has to be Clive and Shay."

"They're here with you?" she asked.

"Yes."

"How did you find out what was going on?"

"Brian's memory came back. And he remembered hearing Tom's voice multiple times while he was held captive."

"Oh, wow." The realization hit her hard. If Brian's memory hadn't returned, she might be dead right now. Quickly she pushed those negative thoughts out of her mind and focused on the positive. Max squeezed her hand. "Where is Tom?"

"Elena has him in custody. He's going to

have a lot to answer for. I'm not even sure what all he's done for East River over the years."

Clive and Shay walked up to them. "Are you two okay?" Clive asked.

"Yes. Rick had Sydney by the throat, but I was able to get off a shot. He's dead and Sydney will need some medical attention."

"I don't want to go to the hospital," she said quietly.

"Please, Syd. Just get checked out."

She nodded reluctantly. With Max looking at her with those caring green eyes, how could she say no?

Max paced outside the hospital-room door as the doctor examined Sydney. She had insisted she was fine, but he would feel a lot better once a doctor gave him that report. Plus, she needed the physician to remove the tracking device.

Max didn't want to let it show, but that shot he'd taken in the woods was the scariest thing he'd ever done. Yeah, he'd trained for those types of situations, but not with the woman he cared for being held captive.

He truly hadn't wanted to kill Rick, but he'd done the only thing he could to save an innocent woman's life. There was no telling what Rick would've done if Max hadn't acted.

While he waited, he took a few phone calls

from the FBI and Marshals. The information was starting to be pieced together because Tom was talking, but it would be a while until they had all the answers.

Checking his watch, he paced nervously outside the room hoping Sydney had no permanent damage to her throat. Her voice had sounded so raspy after what Rick had done.

The exam-room door finally opened and the doctor exited. She smiled at him. "You must be Max. I'm Dr. Stofer. Sydney's asking for you."

"How is she?" He gripped his hands together waiting for her to answer.

"Badly bruised, but I don't think there is any long-term damage. She'll need rest, though, and plenty of fluids. I've also asked her not to overuse her vocal cords for a few days."

"I'll make sure she doesn't." He smiled.

"You can go in now."

"Thank you." He walked away from the doctor and into the room. Sydney sat up on the edge of the hospital bed.

"Hey," she said quietly. "I'm ready to get out of here."

"I talked to the doctor. I need to figure out a way to keep you quiet and resting."

She smiled. "She's getting my discharge papers ready. Then can we go see Brian on the way out."

"Of course." He grabbed her hand. "Just let me do most of the talking."

It wasn't long before a nurse came back with her discharge papers. Max walked Sydney out and they went up three floors to Brian's room.

Sydney sucked in a breath when they walked in. Max realized the shock she must be feeling, since this was the first time she had seen Brian since he was abducted and beaten. And while he looked a lot better than he had, his face and arms were still badly bruised.

"Hey, you two." Brian smiled. "I am so glad to see you."

She walked to the bed and took his hand. "Thank you," she said softly. Max watched as tears formed in her eyes and then streamed down her face.

"I'm just glad I remembered in time, Sydney. I'm sorry I didn't remember all of it earlier."

"How are you feeling?" Max asked.

"Much better. They're talking about releasing me tomorrow." He paused. "Also, I talked to the police and two agents from the internal affairs division at the FBI."

"Did you remember anything else?" Max asked.

"Yeah. Quite a bit. I think Tom is the one who killed Davies."

"Really?" Max asked.

"Yeah. Davies was trying to blackmail him, and Tom wasn't having it. Davies was expendable from East River's point of view."

Max ran a hand through his hair. "If you'd asked me who in the FBI could've been involved with East River, one of the last names I would've told you was Tom's."

Brian nodded. "I'm right there with you. If I hadn't heard it with my own ears, I wouldn't believe it. Although, I think Tom was the person responsible for dumping me out beside the interstate. By doing that he saved my life."

"I knew Tom struggled after his wife left him a few years ago," Max said. "I just talked to some people at the FBI. They discovered that he had a gambling habit. A severe one. That's how he got mixed up with East River in the first place."

Brian shook his head. "Makes me wonder what all I missed while we were working together. How many roadblocks he put up in our investigations."

"Yeah," Max said. "And don't forget, he encouraged me to leave the FBI and go to the Marshals."

"Speaking of that…are you coming back?"

"To the FBI?" At Brian's nod, Max continued. "I've got a lot to think about."

Brian looked over at Sydney. "How are you holding up?"

"Much better now. I'm ready to move on with my life." She sighed. "I'm hoping East River won't have any reason to bother me with Rick gone."

"I think you'll be fine," Brian said. "And if we catch a break, we may be able to bring down Lucas Jones in all of this, too. I'm guessing Tom will try to cut a deal in exchange for his testimony against Lucas."

"You're right. My FBI contact says he's already talking," Max said. "And it looks like that in exchange for a deal, Tom will testify and turn over evidence tying Jones to Kevin Diaz. Tom has already confirmed that Diaz has been funding Jones and East River for years. In return, East River would take care of Diaz's dirty work. It was a mutually beneficial relationship. And it had a solid cover because of the supposed falling-out that the cousins had years ago. This would be a huge takedown for the FBI."

"So if all goes according to plan, Kevin Diaz won't be a free man much longer," Brian said.

"That's good news," Sydney said.

Knowing he needed to allow his friend and Sydney time to rest, Max prepared to leave. "If you need a ride home from the hospital tomorrow just call me," he offered.

"Thanks, man. I'm so glad you're both okay."

Max nodded. "Me, too."

After they walked out of Brian's hospital room, Max turned to her. "You ready to get out of here?"

"Yes, Max. I'm ready to put this behind us."

He led her down a corridor toward the end of the hall where they could have a minute of privacy. He couldn't wait any longer to open up to her. He turned to her and grabbed her hands. "Syd, I was afraid out there in those woods. I had so many regrets that I hadn't come out and told you exactly how I feel about you." He paused. "I thought about losing you and how that would impact my life. Because somewhere along the way, you became much more than just a trusted friend to me. You've become a part of my life. Taking up a huge place in my heart. I can't stand the thought of going back to who I was before we met."

She nodded. "Max, I was afraid, too. I knew that I might not make it out of there alive. And when I thought I was going to die, one of my only regrets was that I wouldn't have a chance to see you again. To actually explore my feelings for you. To live my life to the fullest with you in it." She took a breath. "I am so thankful that you came for me."

"I'll always be there for you. And that's why

I wanted to tell you now and not wait a minute longer."

"Tell me what?"

"Sydney Berry, I love you. I love you with all that I am. You make me want to be a better man. You've given me a precious gift by guiding me back to my faith when I was so hard hearted. My heart is no longer hard. It's filled with love for you. Only you. I don't ever want to let you go." He let go of her hands and cradled her face in his hands. He felt the warm tears stream down her cheeks.

She smiled through the tears. "These are tears of joy. Pure joy because of what I've found in you. After Rick, I told myself I could never trust a man again. That I would never find real love. That I would never find someone who understood me and wanted to be with me. And then God sent you into my life. I care enough about you to get past my fears. There's a hope for a normal life that I never thought would be possible. I love you, Max."

He pressed his lips to hers in a warm kiss. "I love you, too, Syd. I'm not going to say that life with me will be easy and without challenge, but I know we can get through anything as long as we're facing it together."

EPILOGUE

The past six months had passed by in a blur. But throughout it all, one thing was perfectly clear to Sydney. She was in love with Max Preston. Totally and completely.

They'd taken things slowly since he'd rescued her from Rick, but their relationship was growing stronger by the day.

Max said he had a surprise for her today, so she arrived at his house wondering what he had planned.

He opened the door smiling and looking incredibly handsome.

"Come on in."

"So what's going on?" She stepped into the living room and faced him.

"Syd, I know how much you loved your cat, Bach." He led her to the couch where they sat down. "First, I wanted to let you know that I did some investigating and found out that Bach got adopted after he recovered and is doing really well in his new home."

"Max, that is so thoughtful."

"But that's not the only reason I asked you to come over."

She smiled at him. "You're really building up the anticipation here."

He stood up. "Close your eyes for a minute. I promise I'll be right back."

Her heartbeat sped up as she wondered what the surprise was, but she did as he asked and closed her eyes.

"No peeking." He laughed.

Just a few moments later she could hear footsteps coming back into the living room.

"Okay, Syd, open your eyes."

Standing in front of her was Max holding a small furry black kitten. She felt tears instantly fill her eyes. "Oh, Max."

"I thought you were ready for a new addition. I wanted you to name him, but I adopted him from the animal shelter."

"He's mine?" She took a step closer.

"I hope he's ours."

And that's when she saw it. Hanging from the tiny blue collar around the kitten's neck was something sparkly, and it wasn't a nametag. No, it was a ring.

Max handed her the kitten who meowed loudly. Then he dropped to one knee.

"Sydney Berry, I love you more than I ever thought would be possible. I want to make a life with you. A family, starting with this precious kitten and then our children. You're the only woman for me. Will you make me the happiest man on this earth and marry me?"

As she looked down into his eyes, she knew there was only one answer. "Yes, Max. I will."

"No looking back."

The kitten purred loudly in her arms as Max stood and removed the ring from his collar. He slid the diamond onto her finger. Then he sealed the proposal with a kiss.

* * * * *

Dear Reader,

Thanks for reading! *Expert Witness* is my second Love Inspired Suspense, and I enjoyed writing these characters and watching their story come to life. Sydney was an amazing character to write. Even after living through a violent past, she persevered. While most women will not face down their abusers in a physical way like Sydney did, I think her story is powerful. Her physical abilities weren't nearly as important as her inner strength—a strength that grew out of faith. It wasn't easy and took time, but she was able to move on with her life in a meaningful way. Her past may have shaped her, but it didn't trap her.

I hope that you found this story to be filled with faith, hope and love. Again, thank you for reading *Expert Witness*. I would love to hear from you! You can visit my website at www.racheldylan.com, or email me at rachel-dylanauthor@gmail.com.

Rachel Dylan

LARGER-PRINT BOOKS!

GET 2 FREE
LARGER-PRINT NOVELS
PLUS 2 FREE
MYSTERY GIFTS

Love Inspired®

Larger-print novels are now available...

LILP15

REQUEST YOUR FREE BOOKS!
2 FREE WHOLESOME ROMANCE NOVELS
IN LARGER PRINT
PLUS 2
FREE
MYSTERY GIFTS